Abigail Gordon loves to write about the fascinating combination of medicine and romance from her home in a Cheshire village. She is active in local affairs, and is even called upon to write the script for the annual village pantomime! Her eldest son is a hospital manager, and helps with all her medical research. As part of a close-knit family, she treasures having two of her sons living close by, and the third one not too far away. This also gives her the added pleasure of being able to watch her delightful grandchildren growing up.

Books by Abigail Gordon

Mills & Boon Medical Romance

Heatherdale's Shy Nurse
Christmas Magic in Heatherdale
Swallowbrook's Wedding of the Year
Marriage Miracle in Swallowbrook
Spring Proposal in Swallowbrook
Swallowbrook's Winter Bride
Summer Seaside Wedding
A Father for Poppy

Visit the Author Profile page
at millsandboon.co.uk for more titles.

For Glenn, Emma, and healthcare in all its many forms

Glenn's spirits rose as he caught his first glimpse of Emma, coming out of the cloakroom having dispensed with her warm winter coat.

How could he not want her? Emma was special—dark-haired, with smooth creamy skin, curves in all the right places—and tonight she was bewitching, in a black dress with silver trimmings.

So why couldn't he tell her he was sorry about what he'd said on the way home from being stuck in the snow? Why couldn't he give them both a chance to get to know one another better?

Dear Reader,

We are in Glenminster again, surrounded by the green hills of Gloucestershire. *His Christmas Bride-to-Be* is my second book in this series, in which I hope you will enjoy making the acquaintance of Glenn and Emma.

Both have known heartbreak, and both discover that love is waiting to bring joy back into their lives—as it so often does.

With best wishes for happy reading,

Abigail Gordon

HIS CHRISTMAS BRIDE-TO-BE

BY
ABIGAIL GORDON

MILLS & BOON

First published in Great Britain 2015
by Mills & Boon, an imprint of Harlequin (UK) Limited,
Eton House, 18-24 Paradise Road, Richmond, Surrey, TW9 1SR

© 2015 Abigail Gordon

ISBN: 978-0-263-26065-6

CHAPTER ONE

THE TAXI THAT had brought her from the airport had gone, and surrounded by the baggage that contained her belongings Emma took a deep breath and looked around her.

When she'd been driven through the town centre it had been as if nothing had changed while she'd been gone for what seemed like a lifetime. The green hills of Gloucestershire still surrounded the place where she'd been born and had never imagined leaving. Everywhere the elegant Regency properties that Glenminster was renowned for still stood in gracious splendour to delight the eye, while, busy as always, the promenades and restaurants had shown that they still attracted the shoppers and the gourmets to the extent that they always had.

All that she had to do now was turn the key in the lock, open the door and step inside the property that had been her home for as long as she could remember, and of which she was now the sole owner. The act of doing so was not going to be easy. It felt like only yesterday that she had fled in the night, heartbroken and bewildered from what she'd been told, as if the years she'd spent in a land far away had never happened.

During all that time there had been no communication between herself and the man she'd always thought was her father, and now he was gone. Since receiving the news that he had died, all the hurts of long ago had come back. What he had done to her had been cruel. He'd taken away her identity; made her feel like a nobody. Turned the life she'd been living happily enough for twenty-plus years into nothingness.

He had been a moderate parent, never very affectionate, and she'd sometimes wondered why. He'd provided the answer to that by telling her on the night she'd left Glenminster in a state of total hurt and disbelief that he wasn't her father, that he'd married her mother to give her the respectability of having a husband and a father for her child when it was born as the result of an affair that was over.

Emma had directed the taxi driver to take her to lawyers in the town centre where the keys for the house had been held in waiting for when she made an appearance. Once she had received them she had been asked to call the following day to discuss the details of Jeremy Chalmers's will.

She'd been informed previously that he'd left her the house, or she wouldn't have intended going straight there on her return. She was uncertain if she would be able to live in it for any length of time after her father had disowned her that night long ago in such a cruel manner, but it would be somewhere to stay in the beginning while she slotted herself back into life in Glenminster.

Back in the taxi once more, having been given the house keys, she'd given the driver the directions for the last lap of her journey back to her roots and had thought grimly that it was some homecoming.

Gazing down at the keys, the memory was starkly clear of how she'd packed her cases and left the place that was dear to her heart that same night, intending to start a new life to replace the one that Jeremy Chalmers had shattered and made to sound unclean.

Her only thought as she'd driven out of the town that lay at the foot of the Gloucestershire hills had been to go where she could use her medical skills to benefit the sick and suffering of somewhere like Africa and start a new life as far away as she could get.

Until then they had been contained in the role of a junior doctor in a large practice in the place where she had been happy and content, but that night the urge to leave Glenminster had been overwhelming.

The last thing Emma had done before departing had been to drop a note off at the home of Lydia Forrester, the practice manager, to explain that she was about to do something she'd always wanted to do, work in Africa for one of the medical agencies, and that had been it without further explanation.

* * *

Time spent out there had been a lot of things, fulfilling, enlightening, exhausting and *lonely*. If she stayed and went back to work in the practice that she'd known so well in the busy town centre, would the memory of that night come crowding back, she asked herself, or would it be like balm to her soul to be back where she belonged and lonely no more?

Yet was *that* likely to be the case in the house where it had happened and which was just a short distance from the surgery where her stepfather had been senior doctor?

Emma had joined the staff there as soon as she'd got her degree in medicine and had been carefree and happy until that awful day. The job had absorbed her working hours and mixing happily with her own age group in her free time had made up for the atmosphere at home, where there had just been Jeremy Chalmers and herself, living in separate vacuums most of the time.

She'd lost her gentle, caring mother too soon and had been left with only him as family—a bridge-playing golf fanatic in his free time, and at the surgery a popular GP with an eye for the opposite sex. He had proved how much on the night when he'd told her that she was going to have to move out, find herself somewhere to stay, as he was getting married again and his new wife wouldn't want her around.

'Fine,' she'd told him, quite happy to find a place of her own to settle in, but the way he'd said so uncaringly that he was going to replace her mother and that *she* was in the way had rankled and she'd said, 'I *am* your daughter, you know!'

He'd been to the golf club and had told her thickly, 'That is where you're wrong. I married your mother to give her respectability and you a father figure. You're not mine.'

'What?' she'd cried in disbelief. 'I don't believe you?'

'You have to. You've no choice,' he'd said, and added, turning the knife even more as he'd begun to climb the stairs, 'She never told me who your father was, so you can't go running to him.'

As the door swung back on its hinges at last, reality took over from the pain-filled past. Nothing had changed, Emma thought as she went from room to room. There had been no modernisation of any kind.

The new bride must have been easy to please. So where was she now that her father had died from a heart attack on the golf course? It was all very strange. Had the widow moved out at the thought of a new owner appearing?

It would be time to be concerned about that when she'd spoken to the person who had taken over the running of the practice after her father's death. The absence of the new woman who had been in his life could be shelved until she, Emma, had been brought up to date with the present situation there.

But first, before anything else, there was the matter of arranging a suitable farewell for the man she'd thought, for most of her life, was her father. Jeremy had been well known in the town and there would be many wanting to show their respects.

The first she had heard about his death had been a month after the event, when the organisation she was working for had contacted her in a remote region of Africa to inform her of it and had explained that back in the UK her presence was required to organise the funeral as she was his only heir and would need to be the executor of his will.

It was a chilly afternoon, winter was about to take over from a mellow autumn, and having become accustomed to tropical heat Emma was grateful to discover that it was warm inside the house with the old-fashioned radiators giving out welcome heat.

Once her unpacking was finished hunger began to gnaw at her and when she looked in the refrigerator she found it was stocked with the kind of food that had become just a memory while working in the heat and dust of Africa.

It was a comforting moment. Someone had been incredibly thoughtful and had pre-empted her needs on arriving back home in such sad and gloomy circumstances, yet who had it been? There had been no evidence of anyone living there as she'd unpacked her clothes.

It was a Friday, and once she'd been to the law firm the following morning the weekend was going to be a long and empty affair until she'd got her bearings. With that thought in mind she wrapped up warmly, which wasn't the easiest of things to do as all her clothes were for a hotter climate, and decided to walk the short distance to the practice in the town centre before it closed to see if there was anyone left on the staff that she knew.

The darkness of a winter night was all around Emma by the time she got there and the surgery was closed with just an illuminated notice board by the doorway to inform the public what the opening hours were and what numbers to ring in an emergency.

As she turned away, about to retrace her steps, a car door slammed shut nearby and in the light of a streetlamp and the glare coming from the windows of a couple of shops that were still open she saw a man in a dark overcoat with keys in his hand walking towards the practice door with long strides.

On seeing her, he stopped and said briskly, 'The surgery is closed, as you can see. It will be open again at eight-thirty tomorrow morning and will close at twelve, it being Saturday. So can *I* help you at all?'

'Er, no, thank you, I'm fine,' she told him, taken aback by his manner and sudden appearance.

'Good. I haven't a lot of time to spare,' he explained. 'I just came back to pick up some paperwork, and after that have to be ready at any time to welcome back the prodigal daughter of our late head of the practice, which is a bind as I have a meal to organise when I get in.'

Emma was observing him wide-eyed. He was no one she recognised from the time when she'd been on the staff there and she thought he was in for a surprise.

'I have no idea who *you* are,' she told him, 'but obviously you're connected with the practice, so maybe I can save you one of the chores that you've just described. My name is Emma Chalmers. Does it ring a bell? I've returned to Glenminster to take possession of the property that my…er…father has left me *and* to find occupation as a doctor should I decide to stay.'

As he observed her, slack-jawed with surprise, she turned and began to walk back the way she'd come.

It was nine o'clock when the doorbell rang and Emma went to open the door cautiously because her knowledge of neighbours or local people was scant after her absence, so she slipped the safety chain into position before fully opening the door to her caller.

It was him again, the bossy man in the overcoat, on the doorstep and as she surveyed him blankly he said, 'You will guess why I'm here, I suppose.' She shook her head.

'I've come to say sorry for being such a pain when we met earlier. My only excuse is that I have my father living with me and he likes his meals on the dot as eating is one of his great pleasures in life.'

'Er, yes, I see,' she said, 'but why were you, as a stranger, going to be the one who welcomed me back? Surely there is someone still there who remembers me?'

'Possibly, but I am filling the slot that your father left and so was chosen to do the honours. Everyone will be pleased to see you again, I'm sure.'

'Hmm, maybe,' she commented doubtfully, with the thought in mind that there was still the matter of the missing wife to be sorted.

'We had a message from Jeremy's lawyers a couple of days ago,' he explained, 'to say that you would be arriving tomorrow, so back there when we met it didn't occur to me that you might be already here and installed in this place…which isn't very palatial, is it?'

Emma ignored the comment and said, 'I was fortunate when I arrived to find that the kind person with amazing foresight who had switched on the heating had also filled the refrigerator, as I was both cold and hungry after the journey and the change of climate.'

He was smiling. 'Lucky you, then.' Seeing her amazing tan, he asked, 'How was Africa? I'm told that is where you've been. I'm behind on practice gossip as I've only taken over as head of the place since your father died.'

'It was hot, hard work, and amazing,' she said, and couldn't believe she would be sleeping in the house that she had never wanted to see again after the night when Jeremy had removed the scales from her eyes in such a brutal manner.

Her unexpected visitor was turning to go and said, 'I must make tracks.' Reaching out, he shook her hand briefly and said, 'The name is Glenn Bartlett.'

Taken aback by the gesture, Emma said, 'Where do *you* live?'

'In a converted barn on the edge of the town.'

'Sounds nice.'

'Yes, I suppose you could say that,' he replied without much enthusiasm, and wishing her good-bye he went.

Driving home in the dark winter night, Glenn Bartlett thought that Emma Chalmers was nothing like her father if the big photograph on the practice wall was anything to go by. Maybe she'd inherited her dark hair and hazel eyes from her mother, al-though did it really matter?

He was cringing at the way he'd called her the 'prodigal daughter' as he knew absolutely nothing about her except that she was Jeremy Chalmers's only relative, from the sound of things, and his moaning about how busy he was must have sounded pathetic. Would Emma Chalmers have wanted to hear the gripes of a complete stranger?

Yet they were true. Unbelievably, he'd made time that morning to switch the heating on for her, do a dash to the supermarket to fill the empty fridge in the house that she was coming to live in, and put a slow casserole in his oven for his and his father's evening meal.

Back where he had left her, Emma had found some clean bedding in one of the drawers and was making up the bed that had been hers for as long as she could remember, while at the same time remembering word for word what the stranger who had knocked on her door had said.

It would seem that, apart from the father that he'd mentioned, there was no other immediate family in his life, and where had he come from to take over in Jeremy's place? Whoever he was, he'd had style.

The next morning she awoke to a wintry sun outside her window and the feeling that she didn't want the day to get under way because she had little to look forward to except the visit to the law firm in the late morning. Her instinct was telling her not to expect any good news from that, except maybe some enlightenment regarding the missing wife.

When she arrived there she was told that Jeremy's car was hers for the taking in the scheme of things. She felt that explanations were due. It seemed that the man sitting opposite her in the office of the law firm was not aware that she wasn't a blood relation to the deceased until she explained, and when she did so Emma was told that under those circumstances she wasn't entitled to any of his estate, except the house, which he had willed to her when her mother had been alive.

'The car was all that he had left,' the partner of the law firm went on to say. 'There were no financial assets. It would seem that our man Dr Chalmers was something of a high-flyer.'

It was at that point Emma asked if he had married again, as that was what he had been contemplating, and if so his new wife would be his next of kin.

Observing her with raised brows, he said, 'Dr Chalmers didn't remarry, as far as we are aware. Maybe his sudden death prevented him from accomplishing such a thing. So if no one else comes forward to claim the car, it will be yours if you want it.'

Emma left the office feeling weary and confused about life in general.

A time check revealed that the practice building only minutes away would still be open and she decided to stop by and say hello to whoever was on duty, admitting to herself that if Dr Glenn Bartlett was one of them it would be an ideal moment to see him in a different light after being taken aback by his unexpected visit the night before.

He wasn't there, but there were those who knew her from previously and in the middle of carrying out their functions either waved or flashed a smile across until such time as they were free to talk.

As she looked around her Emma was aware that the place had been redecorated since she'd last seen it. The seating and fabrics were new and there was an atmosphere of busy contentment amongst staff that hadn't always been there when Jeremy Chalmers had reigned.

'Emma!' a voice cried from behind her, and when she turned she saw Lydia Forrester, the practice manager, who ran the business side of the place from an office downstairs, was beaming across at her.

'I hope you're back to stay,' she went on to say. 'I've missed you and wasn't happy about the way you disappeared into the night all that time ago. It was a relief to hear from your father's solicitors that you'd been located and were coming home to arrange Jeremy's funeral. He was very subdued for a long time after you left.'

'Did he marry again?' Emma questioned. 'I've wondered who was going to be the bride.'

'Marry!' Lydia exclaimed. 'Whatever makes you ask that?' She looked around her. 'How about us going down to my office for a coffee? They are too busy here to have time to talk. It will quieten down towards lunchtime, and then we can come back up.'

'Yes, that would be great,' Emma replied, and followed her downstairs.

Lydia was silent as she made the drink and produced biscuits to go with it, but once they were seated she said awkwardly, 'I would have been the bride, Emma. Your father was going to marry me. We had been seeing each other away from the practice for a few months and when he asked me to

marry him I said yes, never expecting for a moment
that he would want to throw you out of the house.
When he confessed that he'd told you to find somewhere else to live and that you'd gone that same night
I was appalled and called the wedding off. So, my
dear, you have the missing bride here before you.'

'You!' Emma exclaimed incredulously, with the
memory of Jeremy's hurtful revelations about him
not being her father just as painful now as they'd
been then. 'You gave up your chance of happiness
because of me? I wouldn't have minded moving out,
especially as it was you that he was intending to
marry.'

She couldn't tell Lydia the rest of it. Why she'd
gone in the night, feeling hurt and humiliated, desperate to get away from what she'd been told, but
holding no blame against her mother. She'd dealt
with women and teenage girls in the practice in the
same position that her mother had been in and had
sympathised with their problems.

The practice manager was smiling. 'Your disap-
pearance saved me from what would have been a big
mistake, marrying Jeremy. I'd never been married
before. Had never wanted to, but as middle age was
creeping up on me it was getting a bit lonely and...
well you know the rest. But happiness doesn't come
at the expense of the hurt of others...and ever since
I've looked upon it as a lucky escape.'

'I'm so glad you've explained,' Emma told her.
'From the first moment of my return I've wondered

why the house felt so empty and cheerless. I've felt that I couldn't possibly live in it under those conditions, but now I might change my mind and make it fit to stay here.'

Feet on the stairs and voices were coming down towards them. It was twelve o'clock Saturday lunchtime, the practice had closed, and as friends of yesterday and newcomers she had to get to know crowded round her, for the first time it felt like coming home.

'Where is Glenn this morning?' she heard someone ask, and before a reply was forthcoming he spoke from up above.

'Did I hear my name mentioned?' he asked from the top of the stairs, and as he came down towards them he smiled across at her and asked the assembled staff, 'So have you done anything about arranging a welcome night out for Dr Chalmers?'

'We were just about to,' someone said. 'It's why we're all gathered below decks, but first we need to know if Emma would like that sort of thing.'

'I would love it,' she told them with a glance at Lydia, who had brought some clarity into her life and was smiling across at her.

'So how about tonight, at one of the restaurants on the Promenade that has a dance floor?' Mark Davies, a young GP trainee and a stranger to her, suggested. 'Any excuse for food and fun.'

As the idea seemed to appeal to the rest of them it was arranged that they meet at the Barrington Bar at eight o'clock. As they all went home to make the best of what was left of Saturday, Emma felt that it was beginning to feel more like a homecoming, although she had no idea what to wear.

There had been no time or inclination to dress up where she'd been. It had been cotton cropped trousers and a loose shirt with a wide-brimmed hat to protect her face from the heat of the sun, and any clothes that she'd left in the wardrobe here would be reminders of the hurt that being told she had been living there on sufferance had caused. They would also smell stale.

So after a quick bite in a nearby snack bar she went clothes shopping for the evening ahead and found the experience exhilarating after the long gap of wearing attractive outfits. Her euphoria didn't last long.

There was the arranging of Jeremy's funeral that had to be her first priority after the weekend, and if she'd needed a reminder the amount of black outfits in the boutiques and big stores would have given her memory the necessary prod.

As she made her way homewards with a dark winter suit and matching accessories for the funeral, and, totally opposite, a turquoise mini-dress for the night ahead with silver shoes and a white fake-fur jacket, Emma was remembering that it was the new head of the practice who had prompted the staff to arrange the welcome-back occasion of the coming evening. Would he be there?

Glenn Bartlett knew her less than anyone and, having seen him in the smart black overcoat, she imagined that he would turn up well dressed.

He did come, looking more like an attractive member of the opposite sex than a sombre well-wisher, and suddenly the evening felt happy and carefree after her time of hurt and toiling in hot places.

For one thing, Lydia had solved the missing wife mystery that had been concerning Emma, and for another the surgery crowd, apart from a couple of newcomers, had been delighted to see her back in Glenminster. *And to feel wanted was a wonderful thing.*

The Barrington Bar, where they were gathered, was one of the town's high spots as it boasted good food in a smart restaurant area beside a dance floor with musicians who were a delight to the ear, and as she looked around her the new head of the practice said from behind her, 'So is it good to be back, Emma?'

'Yes,' she said, sparkling back at him, and he thought that the weary-looking occupant of what had been a drab, deserted house had come out of her shell with gusto. The dress, jacket and shoes were magical.

Some of the practice staff had brought partners with them but not so Glenn Bartlett. There was a look of solitariness about him, even though he was being friendly enough after their uncomfortable first meeting.

Did he live alone in the converted barn that he'd mentioned when he'd rung her bell last night? she wondered. Someone had said when they'd all been gathered at the practice earlier that he'd been taking his father with the big appetite home.

At that moment James Prentice, a young GP who had recently joined the practice, appeared at her side and asked if she would like to dance. As Emma smiled at him and took hold of his outstretched hand, the man by her side strolled towards the bar and once he'd been served seated himself at an empty table and gazed into space unsmilingly.

He'd been a fool to come, Glenn was thinking. The fact that he'd suggested a welcome homecoming for Jeremy Chalmers's daughter would have been enough to add to switching on the heating and filling the refrigerator in that ghastly place, without turning out for a night at the Barrington Bar. It would have been a tempting idea at one time but not now, never again.

If it hadn't been for the fact that Emma Chalmers had returned to the Cotswolds for a very sad occasion he would have left her to it, but common decency had required that he make sure she had food and warmth and the pleasure of tonight's gathering to make her feel welcome because she'd looked tired and joyless on her arrival, which was not surprising after a long flight and a funeral to arrange as soon as possible.

Glenn finished his drink and, rising from his seat, told those of his companions who were nearest that he was leaving, going home to enjoy the peace that his father's departure had restored.

Emma was still on the dance floor in her partner's arms and as she glanced across he waved a brief goodbye and was gone.

Back home he sat in silence, gazing out into the dark night with the memory of Jeremy Chalmers's last moments on the golf course starkly clear. He'd known him before stepping into the vacancy that his passing had left.

The then head of the practice and his father had met at university. Jeremy, who had been on the point of retiring, had invited his friend's son, also a doctor, to stay for the weekend to familiarise himself with the running of the practice with a view to taking over as his replacement in the very near future after the necessary procedures had been dealt with.

They'd gone for a round of golf after lunch at the club and while on the course Jeremy had suffered the heart attack that had proved fatal. In intense pain he had managed to gasp out his last request and he, Glenn, working on him desperately as he'd tried to save him, had been stunned when he'd heard what it was.

'I have a daughter,' he'd croaked between pain spasms, 'and I upset her gravely some years ago, so much so that she left to go where I don't know, except it wasn't in this country. Emma is a doctor and most likely has gone to one of the hot spots where they need as many medics as they can get.'

'Bring her home for me, Glenn, back to where she was happy until I told her some unmentionable things about me.'

His lips had been blue, his eyes glazing even as the sound of an approaching ambulance could be heard screeching towards them, and his last words had been, 'Promise you will?'

'Yes, I promise,' he'd told him gravely, and then his father's friend had died.

Now, sitting sombrely in the attractive sitting room of the property he'd bought on the occasion of taking over the practice, Glenn was remembering the time and effort he'd put in to discover the whereabouts of the missing daughter. He was upset to think that he hadn't tuned in to who she was outside the surgery the night before.

Fortunately he'd made sure that the house that had been her home previously was warm and habitable a day early and had had food in the refrigerator. Then had gone the extra mile by suggesting that the folk from the practice make her welcome with an evening in one of Glenminster's high spots.

Now just one thing remained regarding his promise to her father, and when that was done maybe he would be able to have a life of his own once again. The task of locating Emma Chalmers had been mammoth.

He would be there for her at her father's funeral and once that ordeal was over he was going to step aside and let her get on with her life. The same way he intended to carry on with his own, which was empty of womankind and was going to stay that way.

Drawing the curtains across to shut out the night, he went slowly up the spiral staircase that graced the hallway of his home and lay on top of the bedcovers, his last concern before sleep claimed him being the stranger that he had reluctantly taken under his wing.

What was her story? he wondered. Had she been close to Jeremy and they'd rowed about something that had made her go off in a huff? From what he'd said in his dying moments, it had seemed that Jeremy had been the reason for Emma's departure and whatever it had been he'd had cause to regret it.

Since coming back to her roots she had never mentioned him, which was not a good omen, and what about the mother that she'd lost not so long before her hasty departure? What sort of a marriage had she and Jeremy had?

CHAPTER TWO

THERE WERE A few offers to see Emma home safely when the Barrington Bar closed at the stroke of midnight heralding the Sabbath, but Lydia forestalled them by saying, 'I'm in my car, Emma, and haven't been on the wine. Would you like a lift as I have to pass your place?' And added to the rest, 'That leaves two more empty places if anyone wants to join us.'

The offer was immediately taken up by older members of staff, one of the practice nurses and a receptionist, both of whom lived just a short distance away, and when they were eventually alone in the car Lydia said, 'So how has your first full day back in Glenminster felt?'

'Very strange,' Emma told her, 'and unexpectedly pleasant. But that feeling isn't going to last long when I start making the funeral arrangements for Jeremy. He wasn't my father. Did you know that, Lydia?'

'No, I didn't!' she gasped 'How long have you been aware of it?'

'Just as long as it took him to let me see how little I meant to him—which was immediately after he'd said he wanted me gone, out of the way.'

The house was in sight and when Lydia stopped the car she said dejectedly, 'And all of that was because he wanted to marry me? Surely he didn't think I would allow him to hurt *you* so that he could have *me.* None of it brought him any joy, did it? Without even knowing about what he had said regarding him not being your father, I refused to go ahead with the wedding when he told me that he'd made it clear that you wouldn't be welcome around the place once we were married. Sadly, by that time Emma, you'd gone and not a single person knew where you were.

'Jeremy was with Glenn when he had the heart attack and made him promise to find you and bring you back to Glenminster to make up for all the hurt he'd caused you. So he did have a conscience of sorts, I suppose. Glenn, being the kind of guy who keeps his word, spent hours searching for you in every possible way until he finally located you. No doubt once the funeral is over he will be ready to get back to his own life, hoping that yours is sorted.'

Shaken to the core by what she'd been told about the man she'd been going to marry, Lydia was about to drive off into the night when Emma asked, 'Was it Dr Bartlett who saw to it that there was heating and food in the house?'

'Yes,' she was told. 'Glenn mentioned that he was going to deal with those things and you almost arrived before he'd done so by appearing a day early. Now, one last thing before I go—have you enjoyed tonight, Emma?'

'It was wonderful,' she said, 'and would have been even more so if I could have thanked Dr Bartlett for all he has done for me, but as I didn't know about it I shall make up for my lack of appreciation in the morning.'

Glenn was having a late breakfast when he saw Emma appear on Sunday morning, and as he watched her walk purposefully along the drive he sighed. What now? he wondered. He didn't have to wait long for an answer as once he had invited her inside she told him, 'I'm here to say thank you for all that you've done for me, Dr Bartlett. I had no idea until Lydia explained on the way home last night that my father had put upon you the burden of finding me, and that it was you who had made my home-coming as comfortable as possible with food and warmth. It must have all been very time-consuming.'

He was smiling, partly with relief because she wanted no more from him and because she was so easily pleased with what he'd done for her. At the beginning Emma Chalmers had just been a lost soul that Jeremy had asked him to find so that he could die in the hope that he, Glenn, would bring her back to where she belonged. Difficult as the process had sometimes been, he'd had no regrets in having to keep the promise he'd made.

Pointing to a comfortable chair by the fireside, he said, 'It was in a good cause, Emma, and having now met you I realise just how worthy it was. Whatever it was that Jeremy had done to you it was clear that he regretted it. I could tell that it lay heavily on his conscience, and as my last involvement in your affairs, if you need any assistance with the funeral arrangements, you have only to ask.'

She was smiling but there were tears on her lashes as she said, 'I will try not to involve you if I can, but thanks for the offer.'

As she rose from the chair, ready to depart, he said, 'My parents will be at the funeral. They are a crazy pair but their hearts are in the right place and I love them dearly. It was my dad who told Jeremy that I was a doctor and had come to live in the village after leaving a practice up north. So that was how I came to be with him on the day he died.

'Jeremy had been to see me and, having been told that I'd been doing a similar job to his in the place that I'd left, asked if I would be interested in replacing him at the practice in Glenminster as he was ready to retire. Once I'd seen it and been introduced to staff I was keen to take over, and that is how I come to be here.'

'Going through the usual formalities with the health services and the rest took a while but I had no regrets, and now we have his daughter back with us, so hopefully he will rest in peace. You don't resemble him at all, do you?' he commented.

He saw her flinch but her only comment gave nothing away.

'No,' she said in a low voice. 'I'm more like my mother.' Having no wish to start going down those sort of channels in the conversation, she said, 'Thanks again, Dr Bartlett, for all that you've done for both me *and* him.' On the point of leaving, she commented, 'Your home is lovely.'

He nodded. 'Yes, I suppose it is, and with the hills above and the delightful town below them, I am happy to be settled here.'

'So do you live alone, then?' she couldn't resist asking.

There was a glint in the deep blue eyes observing her and Emma wished she hadn't asked as his reply was short and purposeful, and to make it even more so he had opened the door and was waiting for her to depart as he delivered it. 'Yes. I prefer the solitary life. It is so much easier to deal with.'

She smiled a twisted smile and told him, 'I've had a lot of that sort of thing where I've been based over the last few years and to me it was not easy to cope with at all. Solitariness is something that takes all the colour out of life, so I'm afraid I can't agree with you on that.' And stepping out into the crisp Sunday morning, she walked briskly towards the town centre and the house on the edge of it that the man who hadn't been her father had left to her for reasons she didn't know.

There had been no generosity in Jeremy on that

awful night and ever since she had needed a name that wasn't his: the name of the man who had made her mother pregnant. Did he even know that he had a daughter?

Common sense was butting in, taking over her thought processes. So what? You had a fantastic mother who loved and cherished you. Let that be balm to your soul, and as for that guy back there, doesn't every doctor long for peace after spending long hours of each day caring for the health of others? If you've never had the same yearning, you are unique.

Back at the property that Emma had admired, Glenn was facing up to the fact that his description of his home life must have sounded extremely boring. With a glance at the photograph on his bedside table he wondered what Jeremy's daughter would think of him if she knew why he needed to be alone.

Serena was gone, along with many others, taken from him by one of nature's cruel tricks, a huge tsunami, unexpected, unbelievable. Since then he had lived for two things only, caring for his parents and his job, and there were times when the job was the least exhausting of the two.

They'd been holidaying in one of the world's delightful faraway places when it had struck. The only reason he had survived was because he'd taken a book with him to one of the resort's golden beaches and had been engrossed in its contents, while Serena had been doing her favourite thing, swimming to a rock that was quite a way out and sunbathing there.

When the huge wall of water had come thundering towards them, sweeping everything out of the way with its force, they'd both been caught up in it. Glenn had been closer to land and had surfaced and managed to hold onto driftwood before staggering towards what had been left of the hotel where they'd been staying. But of Serena, his wife, sunbathing on the rock far out, she and others like her had disappeared and had never been found.

Weeks later, with all hope gone, Glenn had arrived back but had been unable to bear to stay where they'd lived together so happily. So he had moved to a new job and a new house in the town where his parents lived, telling the older folk that he didn't want his affairs discussed amongst the residents of Glenminster, or anywhere else for that matter.

The only way he had coped after leaving the practice up north to join the one in the town centre had been by giving his total commitment to his patients, and when away from the practice shutting himself into the converted barn that he'd bought and in the silence grieving for what he had lost.

That day on the golf course had been a one-off. Jeremy had persuaded Glenn to join him there for a round or two much against his inclination because it would be interrupting the quiet time that he allowed himself whenever possible.

When the other man had collapsed with a massive heart attack in the middle of the game and hadn't responded to Glenn's frantic efforts as they'd waited for an ambulance, Jeremy had begged him with his dying breath to find his daughter and bring her home to Glenminster. Though aghast at the request, as it had seemed that no one had known where she was, he had carried out Jeremy's wishes faithfully. Once the funeral was over Glenn was fully intent on returning to his reclusive evenings and weekends.

The fact that Emma, having only been back in her home town three days, had visited him on the third one had not been what he had expected. Neither was it what he was going to want once he began to live his own life again.

He'd seen to it that she was back home where she belonged and on a grey winter's day had made sure she would be warm and fed when she arrived. He had even gone so far as to make sure that she received a warm welcome home from the practice staff at the Barrington Bar, of all places, which had not been the kind of thing on his personal agenda. Once his duty had been done he had been off home to the peace that his bruised heart cried out for.

Only to find that Emma had good manners. On the quiet Sunday morning she hadn't picked up the phone to thank him for all that he'd done on her behalf, which until her chat with Lydia she'd had no knowledge of, but had come in person. So why was he feeling so edgy about it?

Was she going to want to come back into the practice? They needed another doctor. But was the daughter of chancer and man about town Jeremy Chalmers someone he would want around the place?

He spent the rest of the day clearing up fallen leaves in the garden and at last, satisfied that all was tidy, went inside when daylight began to fade and began to make himself a meal.

As he was on the point of putting a piece of steak under the grill the phone rang and when Glenn heard Emma's voice at the other end of the line he sighed. She didn't hear it, but his tone of voice when he replied was enough for her to know it would have been better to have waited until the following morning to report the conversation she'd just had with a funeral director.

'I'm sorry to disturb you again, Dr Bartlett,' she said. 'It is just that I've been speaking to the funeral firm, who have been waiting for me to appear with regard to a date for the funeral that has been unfortunately delayed because of my absence, and they pointed out that as my—er—father was so well known in the practice and around the town, maybe a Sunday would be the most suitable day. Then all the staff would be free and more of the townspeople would be able to attend, it not being a regular working day for most people.'

'Yes, good thinking,' he agreed, relieved that the

final chapter of the sad episode on the golf course was to be soon for her sake as well as his. 'Why not call in at the practice tomorrow so that I can help you with the rest of the arrangements?'

There was silence at the other end of the line for a moment and then Emma said haltingly, 'Are you sure you don't mind me butting into your time there? I'm afraid that I've been in your face a lot since I returned.'

Glenn thought that she'd picked up on his morose-ness and his desire to be free of his commitment to a man he'd hardly known, so he told her, 'No, not so. Once the funeral is organised and has taken place we can both get on with our lives.' But as the steak began to sizzle and the vegetables he intended hav-ing with it came to the boil Emma had one last thing to say and he almost groaned out loud.

'Just one thing and then I really will leave you to enjoy your Sunday evening. It is with regard to the food that you provided me with. How much am I in your debt?'

'You're not. You owe me nothing,' he said abruptly. 'It was part of the promise that I made to a dying man.'

Her response came fast. 'So let me make you a meal after the practice has closed tomorrow evening. It would save me butting into your lunch hour to dis-cuss the arrangements for next Sunday.'

His reply was given at a similar speed. 'No! I've told you, Emma. You owe me nothing. I'll see you tomorrow at midday.' And as she rang off without further comment it was clear to her that he was more than eager for the role he had played during recent weeks to be at an end.

Glenn had been looking forward to the meal he'd cooked, but every time he thought about how uncivil he'd been when she'd wanted to thank him for what he'd done for her the food felt as if it would choke him.

Emma would have understood if you'd explained that you still mourn the loss of your wife under horrendous circumstances, he told himself, and that after a week at the surgery you want to be left in peace.

Pushing the plate away from him, he poured a glass of wine and went to sit in front of the log fire that was burning brightly in the sitting room. Gazing morosely at the dancing flames, Glenn admitted to himself that it was most unfair to transfer the pain of his shattered life to a stranger such as her.

He was behaving like a complete moron. Why in heaven's name didn't he explain the reason for his behaviour and try to get it in perspective? Otherwise people would start asking questions that he didn't want to answer.

For one thing, Emma wouldn't want to feel that his attitude was another dark chapter of her life to add to the fact that she had to attend the funeral of a man who had confessed to causing her great hurt.

With determination to atone for the rebuff he'd

handed out when she'd wanted to make him a meal, Glenn decided that he would call at her house on his way home the following evening if she didn't appear in the lunch hour, and do all he could to show Emma that he felt no ill will towards her. That his behaviour came from pain that never went away, so he needed to focus on work.

As his first appointment of the day arrived on the following morning he settled down to what he did best: looking after his patients.

The staff of the practice consisted of Lydia, the practice manager, six GPs with himself as senior, two trainee GPs, who were there to earn their accreditation after qualifying as doctors, and four incredible receptionists who held it all together.

Once the man who had been his predecessor had been laid to rest, the gloom that had hung over the practice might lighten. As a new era began, was Jeremy's prodigal daughter going to want to join the practice, or had he put her off completely? he wondered.

Back at the house the night before Emma had been deep in thought as she'd cleared away after a solitary meal, and they had not been happy thoughts. Did she want to be in the first funeral car on her own? There was no one who should rightly be with her. Her mother had left no relations, neither had Jeremy—and she had no knowledge of who her birth father might be.

Maybe Lydia would join her. If she did it would help to take away some of the dreadful lost and lonely feeling that she'd had ever since she'd been told with brutal clarity that the man she had always thought to be her father, in fact, was not.

The other concern on her mind was the fact that she was having a bad start in getting to know the man who had replaced Jeremy in the practice. She was experiencing a kind and thoughtful side to his character that was contradicted by his brusque attitude on occasion.

It was clear that Glenn was not a good mixer. It would be interesting to find out what sort of a man he was if she joined the practice staff. She did want to feel happy and fulfilled back in Glenminster, if that was possible.

She didn't want to return to the heat and endless toil of Africa until she had recharged her batteries in the place where she had grown up and where she'd had a job she'd loved until the bubble of her contentment had burst.

With those thoughts in mind she presented herself at the practice in the lunch hour. When Glenn's last morning patient had gone, and before the afternoon's sick and suffering began to arrive, he left his consulting room and went to see if Emma had come, as he'd asked her to. He was relieved to find her outside in the corridor deep in conversation with Lydia.

On seeing him the older woman suggested that Emma come down to her office for a coffee before she went, and left them together. So Glenn opened the door that he'd just come through and when Emma was seated on the opposite side of his desk at his invitation he asked, 'So how are you this morning?' He followed it with another question. 'Are you any nearer to knowing how you want the funeral to be arranged?'

Emma was looking around her. The last time she'd been in the room Jeremy had been seated where Glenn was now. The memory of her last day in Glenminster came back so clearly it was making her feel weak and disoriented, although Jeremy hadn't delivered the actual body blow until late that evening, when he'd been drinking and had been about to climb the stairs to sleep it off.

Glenn watched the colour drain from her face and came round the desk to stand beside her, concerned. But Emma was rallying, taking control of the black moment from the past. Managing a wan smile as he gazed down at her anxiously, she said, 'I'm all right, it was just a memory of the last time I was in this room and what happened afterwards that knocked me sideways.'

Straightening up in the chair, she said, 'In answer to your question, I'm fine. I've just asked Lydia if she will join me in the one and only funeral car that will be needed instead of my being alone. I have no relatives that I could ask to keep me company on such a depressing occasion. Obviously there will be other people following in their cars, but that is how it will be for me.'

'And what did she say?' he asked uncomfortably, knowing that he should have given some thought to Emma's solitariness on the day instead of being so wrapped up in his own feelings.

'She said yes, that she will be with me.'

'Good. I hadn't realised just how alone you are, Emma,' he commented. 'If Lydia hadn't been able to do as you asked I would have volunteered. Though whether you would have wanted someone you hardly know with you on such an occasion seems unlikely.'

He glanced at a clock on the wall and commented, 'I can only give you half an hour before my afternoon patients start arriving so what exactly do you want to discuss?'

'I'm going to have an announcement in the local press, announcing that the funeral will be on Sunday at the crematorium at three o'clock, for the benefit of anyone wanting to take part in the service or just to watch,' she told him, 'and I'm arranging a meal for afterwards for the practice staff and any of his close friends.'

'That sounds fine,' he agreed. 'What about flowers?'

'No. Instead, I'd like donations to be made to the Heart Foundation, or locally to Horizon's Eye Hospital, which is an amazing place. Do you think those kind of arrangements will be suitable?' she enquired. She was ready to go and leave him to his busy afternoon, aware all the while that the time she had taken out of his lunch hour might leave no opportunity for him to have a snack or whatever he did for refreshment at that time of day.

But remembering Glenn Bartlett's rebuffs of the previous evening, there was no way she was going to concern herself about that. He was the one who'd suggested a chat in the lunch hour, and in the days when she'd been employed there she'd often missed her lunch due to pressure of work.

'Yes,' he told her, unaware of the thoughts going through her mind. 'Just one question. Am I right in presuming that it will all start from what is now your house?'

'Yes, of course,' she replied, the cold hand of dread clamping on her heart. Until the man she'd thought had been her father had been laid to rest she couldn't even contemplate what she was going to do in the future if Glenn didn't want her back at the surgery.

It was possible, taking note of his manner towards her, that he could be feeling that enough was enough. That having found her and brought her back to where Jeremy Chalmers had wanted her to be... and the rest of it, he'd had enough without her being forever in his sights.

Maybe after Sunday, in the relief that the slate had been wiped clean, she would be able to see everything more clearly. As far as she was concerned, it couldn't come quickly enough. So, getting up to go

down to Lydia's office in the basement for the coffee
that she'd suggested, Emma wished Glenn goodbye
and left him deep in thought.

In the days that followed Emma felt as if she were in
some sort of limbo. She wandered around the shops
for suitable clothes to fill her wardrobe against winter's chill, while trying to ignore signs of the coming of Christmas already on view in some of them.

It was the last thing she wanted to contemplate,
spending Christmas in the house that had been left
to her in its present state. It had always been basic
and she'd often wondered why her mother had never
complained, but now she understood. Maybe Jeremy had expected gratitude instead of requests for
a brighter home from the woman he had married to
save her name.

She supposed she could give the place a makeover or alternatively put it up for sale and move to
somewhere smaller and more modern and not so
near the bustle of the town, but until Sunday's ordeal was over she couldn't contemplate the future.

It was done. The event that Emma had been dread-
ing had taken place and, with Lydia beside her and
Glenn Bartlett hovering nearby, she had coped.
There had been a good turnout, as she'd expected,
and now the staff of the practice and a few of Jeremy's golfing friends were gathered in a restaurant
in the town centre for the meal she'd organised.

Emma was feeling that now the future was going to open out in front of her, though not as an exciting challenge. More as if it was hidden in a mist of uncertainty. As she caught the glance of the man who had brought her home from a foreign country to an uncertain future, she felt her colour rise at the thought of asking for a return to her previous position in the practice. He was so obviously wanting an end to their unwanted connection.

Did he ever smile? she wondered. If his expression was less closed and sombre he would be the most attractive man she'd ever met. His hair was dark russet, his eyes as blue as a summer sky—but always with no joy in them.

It seemed that he was unmarried, not in a relationship of any kind, and lived alone in his delightful property, with the occasional visit from his elderly parents.

Her smile was wry. It seemed as if neither of them was fulfilling their full potential. His life sounded almost hermit-like. Or was it that he had enough to think about with the job and being there for his folks? Although they sounded anything but fragile.

She was being observed in return. What was it that Jeremy Chalmers had done to cause his daughter the degree of hurt that he'd confessed to when he'd lain dying? Glenn asked himself. It had been enough to make her leave Glenminster and only be prepared to return in the event of his death.

Emma didn't come over as the weak and whingeing type. Whatever it was, she didn't carry her sorrows around with her, as he did. Maybe they weren't as dreadful as the burden he was carrying, having Serena there one moment and the next gone for ever. If they'd had a child to remember her by he might be coping better.

The funeral party were getting ready to leave. He got to his feet and joined them and as Emma shook hands and thanked them for their time and their support, he waited until they'd gone and asked, 'Do you want a lift home, Emma?'

She smiled. 'No, I'm fine. Lydia is going to take me, but thanks for the offer. And also thanks once again for the way you have been there for me, a stranger, at this awful time.' Her smile deepened. 'I promise I will not cause any more hassle in your life.'

Before he could explain that his moroseness came from coping with terrible grief every moment of every day, she had gone to where the practice manager was waiting for her, leaving him to return to the empty house that he had turned into his stronghold against life without Serena. For the first time since he had gone to live there Glenn was reluctant to turn the key in the lock and go inside, and when he did so, instead of its comforting peace, a heavy silence hung over every room.

CHAPTER THREE

WHEN EMMA AWOKE the next morning the first flickers of daylight were appearing on the wintry horizon and she thought that it would have been so much easier to have returned to Glenminster in summer, with long mellow days to provide some brightness to the occasion.

The feeling of closure of the day before was not so strong in the moment of awakening to the rest of her life, because in the background was, and always would be, the shadowy figure of the man who was her birth father.

But there were two things to look forward to that hopefully would not have any painful attachments to them. First, the opportunity, if Glenn Bartlett was agreeable, for her to apply for the GP vacancy at the practice where she'd been so happy and fulfilled before, and, second, house hunting for a modern apartment bought from the proceeds of the sale of the house that she had returned to so unwillingly.

With regard to the practice, Glenn couldn't stop

her from applying for the post, but his obvious eagerness to be left in peace after spending so much time on her and her affairs indicated that he might not be bubbling over at the thought of her being still in his life to some extent. The only way to pursue that matter was to get in touch and sound him out about joining the practice.

Before she did either of those things there was something she wanted to do first and that was to put flowers on her mother's grave in a nearby churchyard, knowing that it would have been sadly neglected during her absence as Jeremy hadn't been into that sort of thing.

It had been on her mind ever since she'd come back to Glenminster but she had needed to be clear of her responsibilities regarding *him* before bringing her life back to some degree of normality.

As she approached the grave with an array of winter flowers, Emma stopped in her tracks. It was clean and tidy but already had a display of roses gracing the centrepiece that looked as if they had been put there recently.

The only person she could think of who might have done that was Lydia from the practice. The two women had been great friends and she had called off the wedding when she'd discovered how Jeremy had been planning to treat her dead friend's daughter.

The church was open and rather than not place the flowers she'd brought on the grave Emma went inside and asked the verger if she could borrow a

vase for a short while, and was told to help herself
to any that were standing idle on the window sills.

When she'd arranged the flowers to her satis-
faction and had placed them next to the others, she
stood back and observed them gravely. For the first
time since Jeremy had left her feeling lost and joyless there was peace in her heart and it was all due
to an attractive stranger who had searched for her
high and low to keep a promise he had made.

After leaving the cemetery Emma went to the
garage where Jeremy's car had been kept awaiting
her return to claim it. A large, black, showy model,
it had no appeal whatsoever, and with the manager's agreement she changed it for something smaller
and brighter. She came away with cash to spare and
the feeling that for once everything was going right,
or at least it would be once she'd thanked Lydia for
looking after the grave in her absence.

She had to pass the practice on her way home and
intended to stop to do that, and at the same time ask
Glenn about the vacancy for another doctor.

She found them both having just come up from
the monthly practice meeting in the basement. For
once there was a smile on his face when he saw
her and no sign of the weary tolerance of previous
meetings. She decided that it must be the pleasure of
being off the hook that was making him look happy
to see her. But how was Glenn going to feel if she
wanted to be back in the practice, always around in
some form or other?

'I came to see you both for different reasons,' she told them, 'and won't keep either of you for more than a few moments.'

'Fine,' he said. 'I'll be in my consulting room when you've had your chat with Lydia,' and strolled off in that direction.

'Is anything wrong?' the practice manager asked anxiously.

'No. Not at all,' Emma told her. 'I've just been to put flowers on my mother's grave and there were already some there, beautiful cream roses, when I was expecting it to look totally neglected. I thought that only you would think to do that in my absence. So thank you, Lydia.'

'You're mistaken,' the practice manager told her gently. 'You are right in thinking I had a mind to keep it clean and with fresh flowers, but I haven't done so recently.'

'And you don't know who else might have done?' Emma asked incredulously.

'No. How very strange.'

'Isn't it? I shall have to keep a lookout for the mystery grave-visitor,' she said slowly, 'and will let you know when I discover who it is.'

When she knocked on the door of Glenn's consulting room and was told to enter she was still in a state of amazement. He said, 'What gives? You look as if you've seen a ghost.'

'Not exactly,' she told him, 'but something along those lines.'

'Nothing to do with me, I hope?'

'No. I came to ask if I could talk to you some time about the vacancy for another doctor here at the practice.'

'I see,' he replied thoughtfully. 'So what is wrong with now? The place is empty. We don't make appointments for the afternoon when we have the monthly practice meeting in the morning, so I am free and would like to hear what you have to say.'

'I would like to join the practice again if you would be happy about that,' she told him. 'I would never have left it in the first place if Jeremy hadn't told me something one night that hurt so much I just had to get away to face up to what it meant. I left the next morning.

'It is something I don't want to discuss, but as everyone else in the practice who was present at that time is aware of how I left without saying any goodbyes, I felt that I should explain the reason for my absence to you.'

'You don't have to explain anything to me about your private life, Emma,' he said levelly. 'Mine is buried deep in a black pit that I never seem to be able to climb out of. As to the rest of what you've said, I am concerned that you seem to think I wouldn't be happy to have you as part of the practice. If I have given you that impression, I'm sorry.

'The vacancy has arisen because one of our GPs has gone to live abroad unexpectedly with very little notice. Having once been employed here, you will be aware that in the town centre the pressure is always on. So shall we fix a starting date? And I will deal with any necessary paperwork regarding you coming back to us.'

He was observing her thoughtfully. 'Maybe you should give yourself time to unwind before you come. Your own health is just as important as the health of others, and stress is something that can wind one down into a dangerous state of exhaustion. I know because I've been there.'

Emma could feel tears threatening. The very person she had thought would be dubious about the idea of her rejoining the practice was being kind and thoughtful, so much so that if she didn't make a quick departure she would be weeping out her pain and loneliness in front of him.

'I'll be fine,' she told him hoarsely. 'I need to be with people of my own kind, Glenn, and after the sort of life I've been leading for the last few years nothing I have to deal with at the practice is going to stress me out. Thanks for being so considerate. It is a long time since anyone took the trouble to notice that I was there.' And before he had the chance to make any further comment she went, hurrying through the empty surgery with head bent.

He'd touched a nerve there, Glenn thought when Emma had gone. Had he been so wrapped up in his own sorrows that he hadn't noticed that Emma was not the calm unflappable person that she appeared to be on the outside? The few words of concern that he'd felt obliged to express had opened a floodgate of pain from somewhere. At least he had his parents to give his life some purpose, but there had been no mention of anyone close to her, or surely they would have been at yesterday's funeral.

Lydia knew Emma better than anyone else, it would seem. Maybe she could throw some light on the distress of a few moments ago. He found her on the point of leaving, ready to take advantage of the empty surgery, and asked, 'Can you spare a moment?'

'Yes,' was the reply. She liked the reserved but totally dependable head of the practice. After Jeremy's comings and goings and afternoons on the golf course when he should have been holding the place together Glenn Bartlett was a pleasure to work with.

'Just a quick question,' he said. 'I've had a chat with Emma about her joining the practice in the near future. It seems that she is keen to be back where she belonged before going to Africa and will be with us soon.'

'I am so glad about that,' Lydia said. 'She has had a hard time over the last few years. Emma lost the mother that she adored when she was very young and ended up with just Jeremy in that dreadful house until he upset her so much that she left in the middle of the night. Until you found her no one knew where she was. I am sure she is going to be all right now, Glenn.'

'I hope so,' he said doubtfully, 'but when I suggested that she take some time to recover from the last couple of weeks and have a rest before stepping back into the practice she became so upset I wished I hadn't spoken. Why do you think that was?'

'It could have been because it is so long since anyone showed her any consideration,' was the reply, which was almost word for word what Emma had said.

Lydia could have told him how Emma had been informed that she was a nobody in the unkindest possible way, cast aside by the man she'd thought was her father, and it was his concern for her wellbeing that had broken through her reserve. But there was no way she was going to tell a virtual stranger about the tricks that life had played on someone that she was so fond of.

One of the reasons Lydia had agreed to marry Jeremy had been the desire to be a good stepmother to his motherless daughter, and also she'd been weary of returning to an empty house at the end of each day at the practice.

But he had been his own worst enemy when he'd been too quick to tell Emma that she was going to be in the way when he married for a second time, without divulging the name of his bride-to-be. When Emma had voiced a mild protest, in his drunkenness Jeremy had wiped out her identity, so much so that when he'd woken up the next morning she'd gone.

'I see,' Glenn said, breaking into her thoughts. 'I knew nothing about Emma as she was long gone when I joined the practice. Until Jeremy begged me to bring her back to where she belonged that day on the golf course. Having done as he asked, I have wanted to get back to my own life, such as it is. I will bear in mind what you have said, Lydia. I'm sorry to have kept you.'

'It has been good to talk,' she told him, and clutching her car keys disappeared into the winter night.

He was the last to leave, the rest of the staff having taken advantage of the absence of patients because of the meeting in the basement. When Glenn turned to go to where his car was parked, after securing the outer door of the building in the light of streetlamps, he was reminded of the night he'd first seen Emma hovering hesitantly outside the locked building and had mistaken her for a patient. He had never expected in that moment of meeting that her connection with the practice was going to be the same as his own to a lesser degree.

The thought of it was fine, just as long as his life away from the place was not going to be a furtherance of the responsibilities he had undertaken on her behalf that day on the golf course.

It occurred to him that maybe some shuffling around was required with regard to who was allocated what consulting room. There a vacant one next to his so maybe a transfer for one of the longer-serving members of the practice staff would work, with Emma installed in a room further down the corridor.

As he left the practice Glenn was tempted to call on her to make sure that she was all right after her emotional outburst earlier. He pointed his car in the direction of her house, but drove straight past on observing the flashy vehicle that belonged to James Prentice parked on the driveway.

Trust that one to be first in line when a new woman appeared on the scene, he thought grimly, with the memory of the trainee GP monopolising Emma at the Barrington Bar on the night when the members of the practice had gathered to welcome her back home.

Yet why not? Just because his life was grey and empty there was no reason why those who had a zest for living should be denied the pleasure of it. At least seeing Prentice's car outside Emma's house had brought with it the relief of knowing that she wasn't alone and sad back there after her emotional exit from the practice earlier.

That line of reasoning lasted until he was pulling up on his own drive and knew that he had to make sure that she was all right whether Prentice was there or not. He thought grimly that he really was carrying his promise to Jeremy Chalmers to the extreme. But he was already reversing and when he approached Emma's house once again he groaned at the sight of the same car still on the drive.

But the thought was there that maybe she hadn't invited him, that the pushy Prentice had invaded her privacy for some reason. After seeing him perform at the Barrington Bar the other night there were a few reasons why he had an uneasy feeling about him.

After parking across the road from the house, Glenn rang the doorbell and adopted a casual approach when the door was opened to him, but there was nothing casual about Emma's expression when she saw him standing there.

'Glenn!' she breathed, stepping back to let him in. 'Is everything all right?'

'Er...yes,' he told her. 'I just wanted to make sure that you'd arrived home safely and realise that I needn't have concerned myself as I see that you have Prentice here.'

'What gives you that idea?' she exclaimed. 'I'm on my own. I haven't seen James since that night at the Barrington Bar.'

'But the car on the drive,' he persisted. 'Surely it belongs to him?'

'Not to my knowledge. The only one out there is mine. I did an exchange with the garage on the car that my...er...father left me, for something more trendy. I must have chosen a model similar to that of James without being aware of it as I've never seen his car.'

'Ah, I see,' he said uncomfortably, and followed it with, 'I'm sorry to have bothered you.' He was ready to get off, with the feeling that Emma must be totally weary of him fussing over her like some bore with nothing better to do when his day at the practice was over. Wasn't he supposed to be eager to get back to the days before Jeremy had gasped out his last wishes and placed the burden on him that he'd so wanted to relinquish?

'Have you eaten?' she asked softly.

'Er...no, but I intend to shortly.'

'I could make you a meal if you would let me,' she volunteered. 'I owe you such a lot, Glenn.'

'You owe me nothing,' he said with a wintry smile. 'Except maybe to cherish the life that I've brought you back to with every ounce of your being. Because it can all slip away when we least expect it to.'

With that comment he went striding off into the night to where he'd parked his car. As Emma closed the door slowly behind him his description of what his life was like came to mind. She wished she knew what it was that was hurting him so much, that was responsible for the black pit that he'd described.

But the chances of finding out were slim as Glenn was the most private person she'd ever met. The least she could do was to respect that privacy and get on with adjusting to life back at the practice.

Back home for the second time Glenn was squirming at the thought of the mistake he'd made regarding Emma's car. She must think him an inter-fering fusspot, he thought grimly. If they were going to be working together at the practice he needed to be around less in her private life.

Having been looking forward to the time when he

could let her get on with it, he'd just made a complete fool of himself and it was not going to happen again.

Not in the mood for cooking, he made a sandwich and a mug of coffee and settled down by the fire, waiting for the silence of the room to wrap itself comfortingly around him as it always did. But not tonight, it seemed. The events of the day kept butting into his consciousness and he couldn't relax. The thought uppermost in his mind was that Emma Chalmers was beginning to be a disturbing influence in his life, which was something he could do without. Maybe agreeing to her coming back to the practice was *not* such a good idea.

There were other practices equally as busy as theirs that would welcome her with open arms on hearing the details of where she'd spent the last few years. But would she want to work for them? Had he brought Emma home to places she loved only to want her elsewhere?

The irony of the situation was that he who knew her the least out of the folks at the practice was the one she was having the most to do with. He hadn't intended it to be like that.

But recalling Lydia's veiled comments about Emma's past hurts and the practice manager's obvious desire to have her back amongst them, he was going to have to stick to the arrangement he'd made with Jeremy's daughter while keeping his distance at the same time.

If Glenn had spent a restless evening, so had

Emma. It hurt that he hadn't let her offer him any
hospitality. Not being aware of the chat he'd had with
Lydia after she had left him in an emotional state the
other day, Emma was unaware that his concerns on
her behalf had been brought to the fore again when,
on arriving at her house, he had thought that she had
been socialising with the practice womaniser.

Walking slowly up the stairs to bed with the rest-
lessness still upon him, Glenn stood in front of his
and Serena's wedding picture on the dressing table
and asked gently of his smiling bride 'Why couldn't
you have stayed on the beach, you crazy woman?'

The next morning, with Emma's time her own until
a date had been fixed for her to start at the practice,
she went to check if the strange flowers were still
on the grave beside the ones she'd put there. On discovering that they were, she decided that they were
a one-off of some kind, and once faded would not
be replaced.

With that reassurance in mind she went on her
way to her next important errand, which was regarding house prices in the area. She came away having
surprisingly developed a yearning to stay where she
was and create something beautiful out of her house
during the long winter months.

Glenminster was busy with early Christmas shoppers and Emma didn't want to linger too long anywhere near the practice with the memory of her visit
the previous day. So she parked the car and went for

a coffee in a bistro on the other side of town, where she sat hunched at one of the tables, drinking the steaming brew and digesting mentally the idea of giving a makeover to the drab place that was still her home and so convenient for the practice.

Just thinking about the two places made her impatient to be involved with them both. As if Glenn had read her mind, there was a brisk message waiting for her when she got back to ask how about her returning to the practice the following Monday. For the first time in what seemed like an eternity bells of joy rang in her heart.

She rang back immediately with a reply of just two words, 'Yes! Please!' And for the first time since meeting him she heard him laugh.

'That's good, then,' he told her. 'We look forward to seeing you on Monday next, if not before.' And was gone.

She spent the rest of the day with literature she'd picked up from a local builder while out and about earlier. The ideas suggested for modernising old properties were fascinating, so much so that it was evening before she knew it and Lydia was knocking on her door on her way home from the practice with the news that there were fresh flowers on the grave that hadn't been there the day before.

'After what you told me yesterday I took a stroll through the churchyard in the lunch hour and there they were,' she said.

'But I was there myself first thing!' Emma exclaimed.

'So it must have been after that. When you'd been and gone,' Lydia reasoned. 'But why now, when there was nothing like that all the time you were away? I used to put flowers on occasionally but there were never any others already in place.'

'Glenn goes through the churchyard as a short cut, instead of driving there, when he goes to visit old Mrs Benson. He might have seen someone bring the flowers. Shall I ask him?'

'No,' Emma said uncomfortably. 'I'll keep a lookout myself, he has been involved enough with my affairs and I think is weary of the hassle.' Then she took a leap in the dark. 'Why does he refer to his life so miserably, Lydia? What do you know about him?'

'Nothing,' was the reply. 'Nothing at all regarding his private life, but what I see on the job is a different thing. Glenn Bartlett is the best head of the practice ever. I've seen a few mediocre ones come and go in my time, including Jeremy.

'Which reminds me, Emma, do you have the urge to change your name from the one you thought was yours, considering the heartbreak he caused you, or stay with it to avoid questions?'

'What would be the point of changing it now?' she asked flatly, 'I could always change it to my mother's maiden name, I suppose, but everyone knows me as Chalmers. And as I haven't a clue what my birth fa-

ther's name is or was, I can scarcely change it to that.
If I ever found out, that would be the time to decide.'

'Yes, I guess so,' Lydia agreed, and on the point
of departing suggested quizzically, 'With regard to
what I came about, we will have to take turns watching out for the phantom flower-bringer, I'm afraid.'

'It will be someone who is putting flowers on the
wrong grave and will realise their mistake sooner
or later,' Emma said firmly, having no wish to discuss the matter further, and when Lydia had gone
she picked up the brochures on home conversions
once more.

But her concentration had diminished with the
memory of Lydia's comments about Glenn now uppermost in her mind, and her eagerness to be back
working in the practice overwhelmed her. Just seven
days to go and she would be back where she'd been
happiest amongst those of a like kind, and with her
boss, the man who had brought her back to Glenminster. What more could she ask?

Over the next week Emma didn't hear from Glenn.
And as the days passed, with no glimpses of him
driving past on his home visits, or signs of him anywhere in the vicinity of the house where he lived
the quiet life away from the surgery, Emma found
she missed him. So by the time Monday morning
came she was surprised how much she wanted to
see him again.

She was to be disappointed. There was no sign

of him in the practice building and Lydia met her
with the news that Glenn was taking a break and
would be back in a week's time. With a doctor short,
her presence would be welcomed by the rest of the
staff. As Lydia pointed out the consulting room that
would be hers, Emma thought they wouldn't exactly
be tripping over each other when he did put in an
appearance, as it was just about as far away from
his as it could be.

But there was no time for wishing and wondering.
No sooner had she settled herself and her belongings in the room that was to be hers than patients
allotted to her by the receptionists were beginning
to appear. She had a warm welcome for those she
knew and a cautious approach for those she didn't,
and the time flew with her disappointment regarding Glenn's absence forgotten.

But it returned at six o'clock with the switching
off the lights and the locking of the doors. As Emma
drove home in winter darkness there was the question of why, when Glenn had rung to tell her that
she could start back at the practice today and that he
would see her then, he hadn't kept his word.

Where was he and who was he with? she pon-
dered. None of the rest of the staff had shown surprise at his absence so it must have been general
knowledge to everyone except her that he would
not be there on her first day back to welcome her as
promised. But after all why should she know? She

was just an additional staff member, a new member of the team, no one of particular importance.

The sea was calm, unbelievably so, but all his memories of it were of a gigantic wall of water sweeping everyone and everything before it into total destruction.

The rock where Serena had gone to sunbathe still rose majestically out of clear blue water, just as it had done on that day when his life had changed for ever.

The rebuilding of the hotel where he and Serena had been staying was finished. It had taken three years to make it fit to live in again and the same applied to the rest of the resort that had been their favourite holiday venue.

At long last he was coming to terms with what he had always felt to be the unfairness of being left to live the empty life that had been thrust upon him. He'd been back a few times since it had happened, looking for solace, for answers that might make his life worth living again, but none had ever been forthcoming. Even the strange friendship with Emma Chalmers, which had come out of nowhere and was pleasing enough in its own up-and-down sort of way, wasn't enough to take away the pain of loss.

She had been forced to cope with a loss of her own in the short time since he'd brought her back from Africa, but hadn't felt much grief as far as he could see.

He would be flying back home in the next few

hours, feeling guilty at having not kept his promise to be there on her first day back at the practice. An early morning news item a week ago had alerted him to the fact that the rebuilding of the devastated holiday resort was complete. And that those who had lived there and lost everything in the disaster were returning in the hope that soon the tourist trade would be back and flourishing.

On hearing it, Glenn's first thought had been that he never wanted to go there again. But there had been others that followed it, the most overwhelming one being that he needed to say goodbye to the place, and with it his farewell to the wife he had lost so tragically.

His father had once given him good advice, unwanted at the time. 'Let her go, Glenn. Serena wouldn't want you to live a life of loneliness and grief,' Jonas had urged, but Glenn had ignored him. It was only today, seeing the sea calm and still, the buildings rebuilt and the gardens back to their previous glory, where there had been carnage, that had finally given him the will to let go.

They were waiting for him at the airport, the parents that he loved, elderly and temperamental but mostly on his wavelength. Typically his father's first comment was, 'You left that young daughter of Jeremy's high and dry on her first day back at the practice. Did you forget?'

'No. I didn't,' he told him. 'It was just that when

I heard about the rebuilding on the six o'clock news that morning I knew I had to go. Everything else seemed blurred and vague, and I got the first flight of the day out there. I will speak to Emma in the morning and I'm sure she will understand.'

'And?' his mother interrupted gently. 'How did it feel to see it all made good again? Was the rock still there?'

'Yes, it was,' he told her, 'and it was strange because seeing it comforted me. I felt that at last I could say my goodbyes to Serena.'

'And you'll have a word with that girl of Jeremy's tomorrow?' his father insisted, tactless to the last.

'Yes, of course. I've said I will, haven't I?' he told him as the three of them boarded a waiting taxi. Emma wasn't going to lose any sleep over his absence, he thought. It was the job she coveted, not a washed-out widower like him.

But the time he'd just spent in a place that would be in the background of his life for ever had been well worth the effort. He was ready to accept what he had been given, make the best of it, and it was a major step forward. It was a pity that his father couldn't see it that way, instead of fussing about what he saw as letting down a comparative stranger.

It seemed that he had gone to the practice to pick up a prescription and seen Emma's expression when she'd discovered that his son was not around on her first morning at the practice, and like an elderly knight of old had taken up her cause. For heaven's sake, Lydia would have been there to make Emma welcome and young Prentice wouldn't have been far away, that was for sure.

When the taxi stopped outside the neat semi-detached where his parents lived Glenn paid the driver and then saw them safely inside before walking the short distance to his own home. On the way he had to pass the drab property that was Emma's residence and when he glanced across saw that in spite of the fact that it was well gone midnight there was a light on in an upstairs room, and he thought wryly that maybe she had found it easier to find solace than he had.

She was very noticeable with her long dark hair and big hazel eyes, he thought, and now that she was back in civilisation who could blame her if she found some of the men she was getting to know exciting to spend time with.

Yet from what little he knew of Emma it was strange that she should already be so close to someone of his gender after so short a time, if that was the case. And he might have thought it stranger still if he had known that Emma was propped up against the pillows all alone, studying builders' estimates as if there was no tomorrow.

As for himself, for the first time in ages he slept the moment his head touched the pillow, unaware that Emma's last thought before sleep had claimed her had been of him and his disappointing absence on her first day at the practice. It had taken some of the pleasure out of her return to work, but not all of it. She had slotted back in again as if she'd never been away and hoped Glenn would approve whenever he came back from where he had disappeared to.

CHAPTER FOUR

DESPITE THE LATENESS of his return the previous night Glenn was at his desk when Emma arrived at the practice the next morning. Having left the door of his consulting room open, he was watching for her arrival and called her in the moment she appeared.

Beckoning for her to take a seat, he asked levelly, 'So how did your first day go, Emma? Was it up to expectations? I had expected to be here, but something completely unexpected took me to foreign parts and I didn't get back until very late last night.'

'Yes, it was fine,' she told him, 'just like old times, only better since having worked abroad.'

'I passed your house on the last lap of my way home,' he said, 'and saw that one of your bedroom lights was on at that late hour, so it would seem that you are settling in amongst us satisfactorily.'

'Yes, I suppose you could say that,' she agreed coolly, 'if you would class leafing through a pile of builders' estimates as "settling in".'

Ignoring the implied rebuke, he said, 'You mean

you're considering giving your house a face-lift? All
I can say to that is good thinking.'

'It will be my Christmas present to myself.'

He didn't like the sound of that. Surely Emma had
someone to spend Christmas with? It was clear from
the funeral that she had no close relatives.

But it was still some weeks away. There would
be time for both their lives to change before then:
his because of what had just happened in a faraway
place, and Emma's because by then she would have
found new friends and made her house beautiful.

Any other surmising had to wait as there were
voices to be heard nearby, the waiting room was filling up, and as Emma turned to go to her own part
of the busy practice he said, 'I'm here if you have
any problems, so don't hesitate to ask.'

Glenn watched her colour rise at the reassurance
he was offering and wondered if he had hit a sore
spot of some kind. Had she thought that he was forgetting her past position in the practice and hinting
that her absence over the last few years might have
made her less than capable with her own kind?

If that was the case Emma would be so wrong.
There was an air of efficiency about her that showed
she knew what she was about, and he wasn't going
to interfere regarding that.

She didn't reply to the offer he'd made, just
smiled, and as she turned to go to her consulting
room he pressed the buzzer on his desk and the day
was under way.

In the early afternoon Glenn had a house call to make at a farm high on a hillside. During the lunch break he went to find Emma with the intention of suggesting that she accompany him to renew her acquaintance with the more rural parts that the practice covered, now bare and leafless in winter's grip.

He discovered that she was nowhere around and concluded that she'd gone to do a quick shop somewhere in her lunch hour, until Lydia, observing him finding Emma missing, explained that she was most likely to be found in the churchyard.

When he asked why, the answer was that her mother's grave was there, and Glenn was immediately aware of the strange arrangement of her parents being buried in different places, as Jeremy had been laid to rest in the local cemetery.

Not wanting to question Lydia further, he strolled towards the church and, sure enough, Emma was there, arranging fresh flowers on one of the graves, and he wondered why, as there was an abundance of them there already.

When his shadow fell across them she looked up, startled, and asked, 'Have you come to tell me that lunchtime is over?'

'No, not at all,' he said, feeling a little awkward that he was interrupting something special. 'I'm driving up into the hills to do a home visit for my next patient and thought you might like to renew your acquaintance with the green hills of Gloucestershire. They're as beautiful as ever above the Regency finery of Glenminster.

'My mother was born in this place, but when I came along they were living in Yorkshire because of my father's job. She was so homesick they christened me Glenn after the place she loved so much. At the first opportunity he brought her back to Glenminster and they've been here ever since.

'Not me, though. I met my wife when we were both studying medicine up north and when we married we stayed up there content with our lot until it all fell apart and I came back here to pick up the pieces.'

Emma was listening to what he had to say with wide eyes. Was this the same man who valued his privacy, wouldn't let her make him a meal, and now was putting the blame for his peculiarities on to a failed marriage?

'It would be a pleasure to be up amongst the hills again,' she told him, and with a last look at an abundance of cream roses on the grave she turned away and they walked back to the practice building in silence.

Once they were there Glenn said, 'Can you be ready in twenty minutes? Have you had some lunch?'

'Yes,' she told him, and feeling that she ought to explain said, 'The reason you found me beside my mother's grave is because since I've come back I've discovered that someone is mistakenly putting flowers on it and I need to know who they are.

'I thought it might be Lydia because the two of them were good friends. But it isn't and she is just as curious as I am, as I have no relatives that I know of.'

Glenn was observing her sombrely. What was it about Emma that brought out the need in him to look after her? It wasn't because his return to the place where his life had been resurrected a few days ago had made him want to find a replacement for Serena.

That had just brought some peace to the empty shell that he lived in. That being so, as they drove towards the farmhouse high up on the hillside where his patient lived, he felt free to offer his services with regard to the mystery mourner. He said, 'If there *is* someone bringing flowers in remembrance of your mother, we need to find out why, don't you think?'

'Yes, I suppose so,' she agreed. 'Yet it is a long time since she was taken from me, though not to someone else, it might seem, unless they're putting flowers on the wrong grave. The hurt is always there. I loved her so much, but today I don't want to think about the past. I just want to look and look and look at my favourite places.'

'And so you shall,' he promised, 'when we've seen the farmer and sorted out his health problems. You may remember him from before you went away. Does the name Jack Walsh ring a bell?'

Emma swivelled to face him in the confines of the car. 'Yes, his son was in my class at school. What's wrong with his father?'

'An injury while harvesting that occurred during

your absence. Every so often his spine seizes up and he has to go for hospital treatment. He won't make the effort until I insist on it, and with Christmas coming up he will be reluctant to miss the festivities. Luckily his wife, who knows him better than he knows himself, rang to say that he could hardly walk.'

'So who runs the place?' Emma asked.

'The rest of the family,' was the reply as he brought the car to a halt outside a farmhouse built from the local golden stone that was so popular amongst the builders and house owners of the area.

They found Jack Walsh reclining on a couch, watching television. When he spotted Emma he groaned.

'You're Jeremy's daughter, aren't you?' he asked. 'Come back, have you, now that he's gone?'

Glenn watched the colour drain from her face and anger spiralled inside him. 'Dr Chalmers is here to assist, not to be insulted!' he told him. 'So how about a demonstration of your mobility as that's what we're here to observe? Your wife thinks that it's worse.'

As Jack eased himself off the couch and, leaning on a stick, moved slowly across the room Emma was wishing herself miles away. There had been something in his comment regarding herself that had made her cringe because it had brought back the memory of that awful night when she'd fled from her home.

At that moment Mrs Walsh appeared and greeted

them with a relieved smile and the conversation became medical again. Glenn sternly insisted that the regular physiotherapy sessions that Jack had been giving a miss should be started again immediately unless he wanted to be totally unable to enjoy the pleasures of Christmas.

'Your muscle control is very poor, more from lack of effort than anything else,' Emma told him when both doctors had examined the patient.

'Dr Chalmers is right,' Glenn told him, 'so back to the physiotherapy and we will see you again before Christmas is upon us.'

'Aye, if you say so,' Jack agreed irritably. 'It's all right for some.'

When they left the farm it was three o'clock and Glenn thought there wasn't going to be much time for Emma to renew her acquaintance with past memories. 'It will be dark soon,' he said. 'What would you like to do most in the time we have left before we need to return to the practice?'

Her answer was prompt. 'Watch a winter sunset on the horizon.'

'Right, we will do that, but from inside. How about afternoon tea, somewhere with a good view?'

She hesitated. 'Won't we be needed back at the practice?'

'Not for a couple of hours. My father is insisting that I make it up to you for not being around on your first day there.' Glenn smiled as he drove into the parking area of a cosy-looking café. 'So here goes, afternoon tea up amongst the hills.'

They had a table near the window, the food was delicious, and as the winter sun sank below the sky-line Emma thought it was the first time she'd felt really happy in years.

As he watched Emma, Glenn thought that this stranger that he had bought back to Glenminster was very easily pleased. She made no demands, just quietly got on with the life she had come back to, but he sensed that deep down she was hurting and it almost certainly had something to do with Jeremy.

A smile tugged at the corner of his mouth as he compared Emma's father to his own. His was a 'do-gooder', which was the main reason why his mother sometimes threw him out because he overdid it and his concern for others got her down. While she just wanted a pleasant retirement he was busy looking after all the waifs and strays of the neighbourhood. Glenn understood both their points of view.

He sometimes thought that if he could have given his parents a grandchild to love in their old age it would have been different, but a terrifying act of nature had put an end to that dream for always.

As they watched the sun go down he said, 'I am very impressed to hear that you're going to give the house a face-lift, Emma, but it will be a huge undertaking for you on your own, Why did Chalmers let it get so run-down? He was always smartly dressed, had a big car, and was never away from the golf club, so I'm told, yet the house is a mess.'

'It was just a place to sleep—that was how he saw it,' she told him, 'and if my mother ever asked for anything new, he wasn't interested.'

'Yes. I see,' he commented, and thought that all of that went with Chalmers's type. On the heels of that thought came another that he was already putting into words and thinking he was insane.

'If you decide to go ahead with the renovations, I will be only too pleased to help in any way I can,' he said gently. 'You have only to ask, Emma.'

He watched her colour rise as she turned to him in confusion and said, 'I wouldn't dream of involving you in doing anything like that, Glenn. You did enough in finding me and bringing me back home.'

'Yes, well, we'll see about that if and when the time comes,' he said. 'In the meantime, take everything one step at a time.'

What did he mean by that? she wondered. Was it a reference to her impulsive decision to give the house a makeover, or was Glenn aware that she was attracted to him—a lot?

It was time to change the subject, she thought as they drove back to the practice. 'I've loved being back amongst the hills, Glenn,' she said. 'Thank you for taking me with you. I thought it would be just a matter of a house call to a difficult patient, but it was much more than that.'

He smiled in response, and the thought came to him again that Emma didn't take a lot of pleasing.

But how long was she going to be pleased with him safe behind his touch-me-not barricades? He found himself worryingly close to thinking about her in a way he hadn't envisaged before, so bringing a lighter note into the moment he said, 'So can I tell my father that I have redeemed myself for being missing on your first day at the practice?'

'You can indeed,' Emma assured him. 'Today has been my first happy day in ages. I would be totally content if it weren't for the flowers that keep appearing on my mother's grave.'

'Yes, that I can understand,' he said gently. 'We need to do something about it. I sometimes use the churchyard as a short cut so will be on the lookout. And I'm sure Lydia will be keeping a close watch too, and of course you will be. So between us we should be able to come up with an answer sooner or later.'

When they arrived back at the practice Glenn had a patient waiting and Emma was involved with assisting the practice nurses with a cluster of school children brought in by their parents for the nasal flu spray vaccination, and for the rest of the afternoon the happy moments up on the hillside seemed far away. But in the quiet of the evening the memory of the time spent with Glenn was there again and with it the same amount of pleasure.

* * *

During the following fortnight the mystery of the flowers seemed to have gone away and Emma began to think that maybe it had been someone's mistake as no more strange blooms appeared. The only flowers on view were the ones that she took herself and she was relieved to discover that it was so.

But just when she had started to forget about them the flowers reappeared. Engrossed in her plans for renovating the house, Emma decided to ignore them. Not so Glenn and Lydia, who kept watch for a while, but without any success. Eventually Emma placed them on a grave that was always bare, only to find the unknown mourner not fazed by that as fresh flowers continued to arrive alongside her own.

With Christmas approaching and nothing to look forward to socially, Emma was pleased to hear that there was to be a staff party on the Saturday evening a week before the festive occasion. She felt that it called for something special to wear, especially if Glenn was going to be there. Although she had her doubts that he would be.

Ever since the afternoon spent with him up on the hillside Glenn had been distant when in her company and she wondered if he still spent every moment of his spare time closeted in his house. He had referred to the ending of his marriage with cold clarity and she wondered where his ex-wife was now.

Nevertheless, it didn't stop her from buying a

dress that brought out the attractions of the dark sheen of her hair and pale smooth skin, and as the occasion drew near she resigned herself to being an odd one out in the hotel that had been chosen by those who knew the night life of the town, as it was now, far better than she did.

Lydia would be there and had suggested that they share a taxi to get there but had explained that she would be staying the night at the hotel after the party and so wouldn't be around for the home journey.

'But I'm sure that Glenn will give you a lift home if you ask him,' she'd said. 'He never stays over on those occasions. Just puts in a courtesy appearance and once the meal is over expresses his best wishes to the staff and goes back to the peace of that lovely house of his. That is if you don't want to stay long, of course. Otherwise it will need to be a taxi again,' she told her.

'Right, I'll remember that.' She wondered if deep down she really wanted to go. There were decisions to make about the house, alterations that she wanted done as soon as possible. A quiet night in would help to move the project along more quickly, but there was the beautiful new dress. She did want to wear it when Glenn would be there to see her in it...

In the meantime, as the days spent at the practice went too fast and were so busy, Glenn wasn't looking forward to Christmas any more than he had over the last few years. He may have made his peace regarding losing Serena, but the loneliness was still there.

Restless now in the quiet of his home, unable to relax, he knew he had to do something about it, but what? As head of the practice he was committed to going to the staff Christmas party, which was looming up in the near future. He realised with a combination of pleasure and pain that Emma would be there.

Glenn had shopped already for his Christmas gifts to his parents. As was the routine since losing Serena, he would be spending the two festive days with them at their house, with his mother doing all she could to brighten the occasion and his father restless and on edge because he longed for grandchildren and his son never did anything towards granting him his wish.

He had wondered a few times what Emma's Christmas would be like in that ghastly house on her own. If his two days of festivities were heavy going, hers would probably be worse, unless she had something planned that he knew nothing about.

As far as she was concerned, it still upset her that Glenn hadn't let her thank him for his kindness on the occasion of her return to Glenminster and she intended using the approaching festivities to make up for the lapse in some way.

As the days went by she was beginning to feel a loneliness that had never been there before at Christmastime, even while she'd worked abroad. Although it hadn't exactly been joyful in past years, with just Jeremy and herself to share the event with their opposing lifestyles and little in common, it hadn't felt as empty as this, she thought as she wandered around Glenminster's delightful shopping promenades for a gift for Lydia and a magical something to present to Glenn if he would accept it.

On one of her shopping trips she met Glenn's parents, and his father, Jonas, introduced her to Glenn's mother Olivia as 'Jeremy's daughter come back to the fold' and asked how she intended spending Christmas.

It was an awkward moment. Emma knew that he was always on the lookout for waifs and strays and didn't want to be classified as such, but was lost how to reply to the question. Luckily, Glenn's mum provided an escape route by saying that her husband was always looking for helpers with his good works and on Christmas Day was masterminding a free Yuletide lunch for the needy in the town centre.

'I would love to help with that,' Emma told him with complete honesty, 'either by cooking, serving, or helping generally.'

'I'll accept the offer,' he told her promptly with gruff gratitude, 'but only on one condition—that you dine with us in the evening.'

Emma felt her colour rise at the thought of Glenn's expression when he discovered that she was going to be part of his Christmas celebrations—if that was the correct word to describe the foursome that his father had suggested. Uneasy at the thought, Emma made a weak acceptance of the invitation and braced herself for explaining how it had come about to Glenn the next time they came face to face, which turned out to be the following morning at the practice.

Glenn had been engrossed in a report he'd received from the endocrine clinic in Glenminster's main hospital concerning a patient whose calcium levels had been rising dangerously over past months, according to his recent tests. When he looked up to see Emma standing in front of him she looked very serious, so he asked her what was wrong.

'It's about Christmas Day,' she said awkwardly. 'Your father has invited me to dine with the three of you in the evening and I really don't want to intrude, but hesitate to offend him.'

'I didn't know that you were on visiting terms with my folks,' he commented dryly. 'How did that come about?'

'I offered to assist with the Christmas lunch he's organising for the lonely and needy folks around the place, and the invitation to dine with your parents and yourself in the evening became part of the arrangement.'

'So why the fuss? If you don't want to do that, tell him so. My dad is a great guy for organising other people's lives, whether they want him to or not. But he means well and when it comes to the lonely or isolated he excels himself.'

'And is that how you see me?' she said quietly. As a pathetic loner? You don't know the half of it.' And on that comment she went to her consulting room and prepared to face the day.

When Emma had gone Glenn squirmed at the way he'd been so offhand with her. What was he thinking? The thought of her beside him on such a special day of the year was magical. It would help to take away some of the emptiness that he lived with, but instead of telling her how much he needed her he had sent her away after showing little interest in her plea for his advice. And as the morning progressed there was no opportunity to tell her how much he would like her to be there on the evening of Christmas Day.

The flowers were still appearing on the grave and Emma had decided that if in some way her mother was conscious of them and content to receive them, she was going to let the mystery of them lie like a blessing. So that lunchtime she went into the church-yard as she sometimes did and spent a few quiet moments there to calm the confusion of her conversation with Glenn earlier.

As she turned to go he was there, seemingly having read her mind. Observing her quizzically, he said, 'Do you ever regret coming back to Glenminster, Emma?'

'No, of course not,' she said immediately. 'I belong here and nowhere else, but there are unsolved questions I have to live with.'

'Such as the mystery flowers?'

'Yes, that in part; but bigger issues than that haunt me. I envy you your parents, Glenn. You are so fortunate to have them here in your life every moment of every day. Although I am so sorry that your marriage didn't work.'

'Is that what you think?' he exclaimed. 'That I'm divorced or something of the sort?'

'Well—yes, I assumed.'

'I'm not divorced, Emma,' said Glenn. 'My wife is dead. Swept away in a tsunami when we were on holiday some years ago.'

'Oh, how awful for you!' she breathed. 'I had no idea. Do, please, forgive me for jumping to the wrong conclusion.'

'It's an understandable mistake to make,' he said. 'Only my parents know what happened and at my express request they don't discuss my affairs with anyone. It's something I don't like to talk about, and I would be obliged if you would do the same.'

'Yes, of course,' she told him, still stunned by what he had told her. 'I really am so very sorry, Glenn. If ever there is anything I can do to help, do please say so.'

He was smiling a tight smile. 'There *is* one thing. In spite of my having put the dampener on it earlier, how about you sitting beside me on Christmas Day night to please my parents? I'll pick you up at seven o'clock if that's all right.'

'Er...yes,' she replied, wondering what he would say next to amaze her, and asked hesitantly, 'What shall I bring?'

'Just yourself will do fine,' she was told, and with a glance at the clock in the church tower high above them added, 'We had better get back to our patients or we'll have a queue.'

Emma smiled across at him, happier than she'd felt for ages. The invitation to join Glenn and his family for a Christmas meal made her feel more wanted than she had done in a long time. But poor Glenn! What he'd had to say about the loss of his wife was heartbreaking and explained so many of the things about him that had previously puzzled her.

It was the day of the staff party and with that and Christmas the following week, with all the excitement and nostalgia that entailed, there was a lovely heart-warming atmosphere in the surgery. Everyone was looking forward to the festive season and a well-earned rest. It was midday and most of the staff had already gone to enjoy their weekend when a phone call came through to say that Jack Walsh needed to see a doctor urgently. Glenn sighed. Jack had a high temperature and it sounded as if he might have some sort of infection. After checking that the building was empty, he locked up and went to his car, ready to drive up to the remote farm.

At that moment Emma drove onto the practice forecourt and he observed her in surprise. Having noted that her consulting room was empty, Glenn had taken it for granted that, like the rest of the staff, she had gone to enjoy the weekend ahead.

As she got out of her car he wound his window down and asked in surprise, 'Where have you been? Everywhere is locked up. I'm off to see Jack Walsh at the hill farm. He has a high temperature and from what his wife says seems to be heading for something serious.'

'Can I go along with you?' she asked. 'I missed the hills so much while I was away and loved it the other time you took me up there.'

'I would have thought that you'd have lots of nice things planned for the rest of the day,' he said. 'Come, by all means, if you wish, but it won't be much fun up there on a day like this. There is a definite nip in the air and the sky is dark and lowering.'

Emma was already easing herself into the passenger seat beside him and flashed him a smile. 'It's a case of anything to get out of my stately home,' she teased, and he could understand that.

'Where have you been?' Glenn asked as he drove off the forecourt of the practice.

'To see a child with 'flu,' she replied. 'I hope I don't get it for Christmas.'

So do I, he thought. The party later that night and having Emma with him at his parents' house on Christmas Day were beginning to stand out in his mind like stars in a dark sky.

By the time he pulled up at the Walsh farm it was snowing. Large flakes were falling all around them, silently forming a white carpet that was getting thicker by the moment. Glenn said, 'Are you wishing you hadn't come? We could be snowed in up here and it's the staff party tonight.'

The question had an answer that was making her heart beat faster. Emma wanted to be wherever Glenn was, be it the smart hotel where the staff party was to be held or on the Walshs' ramshackle farm, so as Mrs Walsh opened the door, Emma's smile was serene.

'Doctor, he's bad this time,' she said worriedly, as she led the way to a drab bedroom on the ground floor of the building. 'He's hot as fire, his breathing is difficult, and he isn't talking sense.'

'How long has he been like this?' Glenn asked, as he bent over the feverish figure on the bed.

'He's gradually been getting worse since yesterday,' was the reply.

Glenn frowned.

'It could be pneumonia or something worse,' he said when the two doctors had finished examining him. 'I'm going to phone for an ambulance and hope that it will be able to get here before this place becomes inaccessible.' He sent a wry smile in Emma's direction. 'So much for life in the fast lane.'

'I don't mind,' she told him, and she really didn't

as long as she was with him. Although Glenn was still an unknown quantity as far as she was concerned. Since they'd met he'd wanted nothing of her or from her, and as far as she knew nothing had changed.

It was still early afternoon. They might get to the party yet if the snow eased off and an ambulance managed to get through. She would still be able to wear the dress that she'd been hoping would make Glenn see her how she wanted him to.

CHAPTER FIVE

An hour later an ambulance did come trundling through the snow with its siren screeching. After a quick word from Glenn the sick man was taken on board and was on his way to the nearest hospital, leaving the two doctors to get back to civilisation the best they could.

After a mile of careful driving with visibility almost nil the car became stuck in a snowdrift. Glenn had been worried when they'd set off, but now anxiety on Emma's behalf spiralled as there was no signal when he tried to phone for help. He got out to assess the situation and was hit straight away by the severe cold.

'I should never have let you come with me!' he said when he opened the door to ease himself back in. 'I suggest that you climb over onto the back seat and if I leave the engine running you may be able to keep warm while I dig us out of this mess. I keep a couple of shovels in the boot for situations such as this.'

'Give me one and I'll help,' she said immediately.

He shook his head. 'No! You stay put and keep trying to get a signal on the phone while I'm out there, digging.'

As she was about to protest at his refusal to let her assist he said tightly, 'Do as I say, will you?' And she obeyed meekly.

A short time later he got back behind the wheel but had no luck—the car was still stuck. He groaned as he climbed into the back seat beside her and asked grimly if she'd been able to get a signal.

When she shook her head Glenn held out his arms and when Emma made no move towards him he said dryly, 'I don't bite. I am merely offering body warmth because the car heater doesn't seem to be working.'

With a wry smile she went into his hold and as he held her close against his chest, in spite of the snow drifting silently and thickly around the car, she had never felt so safe in her life before. Beside her, Glenn was thinking that it was the first time he had held a woman in his arms since he'd lost Serena and it was arousing all the passions he had kept so tightly under control ever since.

Because it wasn't just any member of the opposite sex he was holding close. It was the daughter that Jeremy Chalmers had confessed to having done some great hurt to as he'd been dying, and he, Glenn, would very much like to know what it was.

'So tell me what it was that Jeremy did to you

that hurt so much,' he said gently, when they'd sat in silence for a while.

Her face clouded and Glenn thought she was going to refuse, but after a pause she sighed. 'He had been out drinking and came home late. Then he told me that I would have to move out of the only home I'd ever known. That he was getting married for a second time and that I was not welcome to stay where I had lived all my life,' Emma said. 'And when I protested that I was his daughter and didn't deserve such treatment, he informed me that he was not my father. He had married my lovely mother to give her respectability, and her child—me—a name. And as a final hurtful truth he told me that he had no idea who my father was, that my mother had never told him, so I was a nobody.

'Unable to bear the thought of staying in Glen-minster after listening to his nastiness, I left during the night and had no intention of ever returning until you got in touch and brought me back to the place I loved.'

She turned, looked up at him from the circle of his arms and said softly, 'I will always bless you for that, Glenn.'

Emma's mouth was only an inch or two away. It would be so easy to kiss her, he thought achingly, kiss away the hurts that Jeremy had caused in his spiteful drunkenness, and make love to her in the privacy of the snowbound car.

Tilting her chin with gentle fingers, he looked

down at her upturned face and it was there, the feeling of togetherness that she aroused in him, and letting desire take hold of his senses he kissed her just once long and tenderly, then it was gone, swept away by the happenings of the past that still had him in their grip.

The mighty wall of water surging towards him that, when it had taken its toll of the holiday resort, had also taken Serena, along with many others, and ever since he'd carried with him the guilt of being spared when she had been lost.

The torment of the thoughts that wouldn't allow him to hold Emma any closer was broken by the sound of some sort of vehicle approaching through the swirling white flakes and she cried, 'It sounds like a truck of some sort, Glenn!'

Relief washed over him, mixed with regret that he hadn't taken advantage of the magical moments when he'd held her in his arms, but her safety had to come first and he said, 'It's a snow plough, Emma. We might get to the staff party after all if they can pull us out of this drift.'

At that moment a voice could be heard across the divide between the two vehicles.

'Are you folks OK?' a voice called. 'The ambulance crew phoned to say you might have problems getting back to civilisation, so we're here to clear the way for you to drive back to Glenminster.'

'Yes, we're fine,' Glenn told them. 'But the drifts around the car were getting a bit worrying, so the

sooner you can get us moving again the more grateful we will be. We're so thankful for your help.
Where have you come from?'

'We're from a farm not far away,' was the reply.
'The police and local council know I have one of
these things and we have an arrangement that I come
out to tow folks like you out of the drifts.' The young
guy seated beside him jumped down onto the snow
with ropes in his hands and attached them to the
front of Glenn's car. 'This is my son. He knows what
he's doing. We'll soon have you free and on your
way.' When the car suddenly lurched forward onto
level ground they knew that it wasn't a vain promise.

As he thanked them before moving slowly onto
the main road that would take them back to the town
Glenn said, 'If ever I can do you a favour you have
only to ask.'

The farmer laughed from high up on the driving
seat of the snow plough and said, 'I could do with
something for my indigestion.'

'So shall we see you at the surgery on Monday
morning, then?' Glenn grinned.

'You might,' was the reply as the man went trundling off into the distance.

On the way back Glenn was silent. Emma wondered if he was already regretting those moments
when they'd been so close, surrounded by drifting
snow with the moment to themselves. As if he sensed
her thoughts he said, 'That wasn't the best drive
back, was it?'

Stung, she replied, 'I thought that some of it was very pleasant.'

'Yes, maybe,' he said, 'but circumstances can sometimes create illusions that are not meant to be.'

Her house had come into sight and when Glenn stopped the car outside he said, 'So are you going to the party? There is still time. I'm going as I have no choice. As head of the practice I have to keep putting in an appearance at these sorts of things, but I don't intend to stay long.'

'Yes, I'm going,' she told him. 'I was looking forward to it, but suddenly it has become a chore.' She felt like telling him that she'd bought a special dress for the occasion, but wouldn't be wearing it after the way he'd put the dampener on those magical moments in the car.

'That's good, then,' he said, ignoring her downbeat comment.

Without her there the event would mean nothing to him in spite the downturn in his mood.

As Emma watched him drive off into the night the memory of being in his arms on the back seat of the car was warming her blood, bringing desire again into the moment.

Yet how crazy had that been, acknowledging their attraction to each other at such a time. The memory came to mind of the Sunday morning when she'd gone to his house to thank him for all that he had done in preparation for her arrival and had asked if he lived alone.

'Yes, I do,' he'd told her, and had sent her on her way with the feeling that he was a loner and preferred it that way. Since then she had got to know him better and, knowing that he had lost his wife in the most awful circumstances, she decided if she let herself fall in love with a man who still lived in the past she must be crazy.

By the time Lydia arrived to pick her up, Emma had changed her mind about the dress. She would wear it after all. Whatever Glenn thought of their relationship, there was no call for her to dress down because he wasn't interested in her. She owed it to herself, if no one else, and was determined to enjoy the evening no matter what.

Glenn's spirits rose as he caught his first glimpse of her coming out of the cloakroom, having dispensed with her warm winter coat. How could he not want her? Emma was special, dark-haired with smooth creamy skin, curves in all the right places, and tonight she looked bewitching in a black dress with silver trimmings. So why couldn't he tell her he was sorry about what he'd said on the way home from the farm? Why couldn't he give them both a chance to get to know one another better?

Yet Glenn found he couldn't. As their glances held he turned away and went to chat to other staff members who didn't have the same effect on him as Emma did. As the evening progressed his only communication with her was to ask briefly if she was all right after the snow hazard they'd encountered. Emma's brief response that she was fine gave him no further encouragement, so he left her chatting to James and wished him miles away.

Glenn got up to leave after the meal and to say goodbye to Lydia and Emma, who were seated nearby. 'Why are you going so soon?' Lydia asked.

'It's been a long day,' he said, his smooth tone covering up his turbulent feelings. 'Has Emma told you we had to be rescued from a snowdrift by a local farmer and his son in their snow plough?'

'Er…no,' Lydia replied, and he smiled tightly.

'Maybe you didn't think it worth mentioning,' he said, turning to where Emma was sitting.

'Some parts of it were and some weren't,' she told him quietly, intent on not revealing the hurt of his comments on the way home.

'Ah, yes,' he said, and looked deep into her eyes. 'I'm sorry if I offended you, Emma.'

'It's forgotten,' she said, and wished it was true. But she *had* felt hurt and there was no way she wanted that to become common knowledge.

Glenn left then, striding purposefully towards the door. Heads turned at the sight of his looks and stature and Emma swallowed hard. His leaving felt like another rebuke in her empty life and she wished she had stayed at home and planned the alterations to her house instead.

'What have you done to upset Glenn?' Lydia asked curiously, breaking into her thoughts.

'Nothing at all,' she said tightly, and added, in a moment of sheer misery, 'Why does no one ever want me, Lydia? First there was my unknown father, who can't have wanted either my mother or me, then Jeremy told me to leave, and now Glenn, who I admire and respect, wants me to keep my distance.'

'I don't know about the rest of it,' Lydia said comfortingly, 'but for some reason Glenn has no wish to settle down, which is a shame because I've never seen him look at any other member of our sex like he looks at you. Try not to be too sad, Emma.'

As she listened to what Lydia had to say she remembered Glenn confiding in her about how he had lost his wife and requesting her not to discuss it with anyone. She couldn't tell Lydia what she knew so without further comment, when James appeared at her side once more she excused herself and let him take her onto the dance floor just once more. Then she rang for a taxi.

On the way home she did a foolish thing. Instead of letting the taxi driver take her straight home, Emma asked him to drop her off beside the church and beneath the light of a full moon made her way towards the grave, curious to see if any more flowers had been left there.

As she drew nearer she saw someone standing motionless beside it and increased her pace. But by the time she got there whoever it was had gone and as the quiet night surrounded her once again she looked down at the grave and they were there again, flowers from someone who must have known her mother.

As Emma walked the short distance to her dismal home she wished that Glenn was by her side and for once her wish was granted. He pulled up beside her from nowhere and without speaking opened the car door for her to get in.

Once she was seated he asked, 'Emma, what happened to the taxi that you set off for home in? Lydia rang me to say that you had left the party early too and she was worried about you. So I went round to your place to make sure you were safe and found it in darkness.'

'Yes, I know,' she admitted meekly. 'It was a crazy thing to do but as the taxi was about to go past the church I had a sudden urge to check if any more flowers had been put on the grave. So I paid the driver and went to see.'

'And?' he questioned.

'There was someone standing beside it in the moonlight, Glenn, but by the time I was near enough to see them clearly they'd gone. When I looked down fresh flowers had been put in the vases.'

'And did you have time to see what gender this person was?' he asked. 'It's unlikely a woman would be found in a churchyard after dark.'

'No,' she told him. 'It is as I said. They'd gone

by the time I got to the grave. Maybe they heard my footsteps on the flagged path.'

'Has it made you nervous?'

'A bit, I suppose, but it was my own fault.'

The car was already pointing in the direction of Glenn's house. Emma sat bolt upright in shock when he suddenly said, 'I'm going to take you to my place for the night. I never feel easy about you being in that house on your own after dark, and just in case the person in the graveyard saw you, or already knows where you live, we aren't going to take any chances.'

'Do you have a spare room?' she enquired faintly.

'Yes, of course I have! I've got two, as a matter fact, and you'll be quite safe in whichever one you prefer.'

'You know that I'll be green with envy while I'm inside your house, don't you?' she teased.

'There's no need to be,' he parried back. 'Like they say, a home is where the heart is and mine is in a place far away.'

Glenn watched the light go out of her eyes and the colour drain from her face and wished he hadn't been so clumsy.

You are crazy to have brought her here, he told himself as he put his key in the lock when they arrived at the converted barn that appealed to her so much. Especially after the way the two of you were up there in the snowdrift. She's beautiful and kind. For pity's sake, don't hurt her because you've been hurt. Emma has had enough sadness in her life already. Don't get involved in promising her something that you aren't able to give.

When he turned to face her, though, he was smiling, and as she observed him questioningly he said, totally out of context, 'The dress is lovely, Emma. Just so right for your colouring. I intended telling you that at the party but the opportunity didn't present itself.' Unaware of what had been in his mind just a few moments ago, she asked a question that he would rather not have had to answer.

'What was your wife like, Glenn?' she asked, and his smile disappeared.

'I have her photograph in my bedroom. If you would like to see it I'll bring it down,' he volunteered.

'Only if you want to,' she told him. He went upstairs and brought the picture back, and as Emma observed the smiling golden-haired woman in the photograph she could understand his abiding affection for her. But if Glenn's wife had loved him as much as he loved her, surely she would have wanted him to find happiness again with the right person?

Her own track record of not being wanted meant that she certainly wasn't at the top of anyone's yearning-for list. She could only imagine that happening in her dreams.

Emma was unaware that Glenn was watching her, taking in her every expression. He felt full of tenderness for her, but someone like Emma deserved better than him. Despite that, as he listened to her telling him gently that his wife had been very beautiful, for once he was more enraptured by a woman other than Serena.

As Emma handed the photograph back to him Glenn said, 'If you'd like to come upstairs I'll show you the guest room. Feel free to get up whenever you like in the morning. It's Sunday, so there's no rush. Would you like a hot drink before you settle for the night?'

'Er...no, thanks,' she replied. 'I had plenty to eat and drink at the party. Glenn, I'm sorry that I've caused you concern by my actions. It was stupid of me to go into the churchyard at that hour. I don't know what possessed me,' she added guiltily. 'I won't stay for breakfast. I'll leave early so as not to cause further disruption of your organised life, and see you back at the practice on Monday.'

'I don't think so,' he said. 'Breakfast is part of the arrangement of you sleeping safe and sound beneath my roof for once.'

It had been a long day and Emma was tired, but sleep was evading her because the events of the day had been so strange. It seemed unbelievable to her that Glenn could be sleeping only feet away in the master bedroom of his converted barn. His last comment before he'd closed the door had been to tell her she would find a selection of nightwear in the dressing-table drawers.

And now wearing a long chaste-looking night-

dress of white cotton that seemed more like something that belonged to his mother than Glenn's
cherished wife, Emma was sleepless still because
the very idea of being so near yet so far from him in
every other way during the night hours was incredible. And in the morning there would be joy in her
heart when she went downstairs and he was there.

Glenn's bedroom door was wide open when Emma
sallied forth fully dressed the next morning and she
smiled at the thought of seeing him. It would be just
two people getting to know each other, sharing their
different joys and sorrows, she thought, and what
could be wrong with that?

What *was* wrong with it was that Glenn was nowhere to be seen anywhere in the house. She went
from room to room with the minutes ticking by, but
there was no sign of him. There was no kettle boiling
or bacon sizzling to create a breakfast atmosphere.

Outside, the drive and gardens were also deserted, and Glenn's car was nowhere to be seen.
The only thing that *was* of interest were brochures
about holidaying in Italy on the hall table, and she
wondered if Glenn was planning a trip abroad.

Surely he hadn't already gone and in a rush to
be off had forgotten she was there from the night
before? It would fit in with how she saw herself as
someone of little importance.

Though why should she be so quick to expect
that he had left her like that? Glenn was thoughtful

and caring. But annoyance was building up inside her and in her confusion she was hurting because he had insisted on her staying the night and now he was gone and she didn't know where.

Reaching for her topcoat hanging up in the hall, Emma gathered the few belongings that she'd had with her from the staff party. Two could play at that game, she thought tearfully and stepped out onto the drive, intending to make her way home on foot. Only to be brought to a halt when Glenn's car appeared. Within a matter of seconds he was out of it and observing her with a questioning smile that was the final irritation of the morning.

'I'm sorry, Emma,' he said. 'You must think me very rude to have been missing when you came down for breakfast.' She observed him in chilly silence. 'I got my timing wrong, I'm afraid. My mother phoned me before daybreak to say that Dad wasn't well. He's got some sort of throat infection and has a temperature, so she asked me to go and examine him.

'As there is rarely anything serious when they ring me on these occasions I went straight away, without disturbing you or leaving a message. I expected to be back within a very short time, only to get there and find him unwell with what seems like tonsillitis.

'So I had to write out a prescription and go and pick it up at an all-night chemist. I have promised to call again later. Could I persuade you to come back inside for some breakfast?'

She didn't say yes or no, just asked tightly, 'So why didn't you wake me up or leave a note? I would have been only too willing to have gone with you and done anything to help that I could.'

'What, after the day that you'd had?' he protested. 'Being insulted by that insolent Walsh fellow at the farm, and then caught in a snowdrift, followed by enduring my miserable comments on the way home?

'I scare myself sometimes when reality hits me. It takes me out of my safe cocoon and reminds me that life has to go on, that I'm not the only one who lost someone they loved on that dreadful occasion.'

He took her hand and drew her gently towards the door, wide open behind her, and once they were inside he unbuttoned her coat, slipped it off her shoulders and, holding her close, asked, 'So what would madam like for breakfast?'

'I'm not hungry,' she told him, stiffening in his arms. She wasn't hungry, for food anyway, reassurance maybe, and Glenn was offering a plateful of that.

'I can't believe it,' he said gently, and planted a butterfly kiss on her cheek. 'How about that for starters, followed by food, glorious food?'

She was smiling now, the feeling of being left out in the cold disappearing, and when they'd eaten and she'd helped him tidy the kitchen Emma went with Glenn to visit his parents. She envied him the closeness of his small family.

If there was just one person *she* could call family and give her love and affection to now that her mother was gone, she would be content. But there was no one.

'You are so lucky to have your parents still with you,' she told Glenn as he drove her home in the quiet Sunday morning. 'I lost my mother some years ago and Jeremy wanted me gone as soon as he found someone to replace her.'

Glenn didn't comment but rage swept over him in a hot tide at the thought of what Jeremy had done to Emma. It wasn't surprising he'd been desperate to go to his maker with a clean slate. As far as Glenn was concerned, the man had done him a favour by asking him to find her, wherever she might be.

But his attraction to Emma was something new in his life and he was going to have to decide where he was going from this moment in time. Glenn would have liked to have spent the rest of the day with her, but once he had satisfied himself regarding his father's condition Emma had explained that she was expecting the builder to call with regard to the alterations she was planning and wanted to be there when he arrived.

'So, until tomorrow at the practice,' Glenn said, as he braked the car in front of her house, and with colour rising Emma thanked him for his hospitality, kissed him lightly on the cheek and was gone, leaving him to go back to make sure that his father really was improving with the touch of her lips against his skin feeling like a combination of a promise and a goodbye.

The patient *was* feeling better, his temperature was down, the inflammation in his throat reducing. Typically Jonas was now in a more upward mood with his thoughts turning to the event he was planning for the old and lonely on Christmas Day and wanting to know if Emma was still available to keep her promise of assisting.

'Yes, as far as I know,' Glenn told him. 'The surgery will be closed so she should be free, unless she has changed her mind.'

'And is she still going to dine with us in the evening?' his mother questioned.

'I suppose the same applies,' he said dryly, and left it at that, knowing that if Emma kept her promise and came to eat with them as arranged, whatever else there was between them it would be the best Christmas he'd had since he'd lost Serena. Which led him to wonder how was he going to make her aware of his feelings. He wanted to, needed to, because if nothing ever came of their attraction to each other, at least she had brought some joy into his empty life.

It was Monday morning and Emma was feeling miserable because the builder's quote for her requirements had been far above what she could afford, but she was excited about something else.

She'd noticed during her stay at Glenn's house that the one next to his was for sale and she'd gone home with an idea. It was of a similar design, though smaller, but just as attractive, and when the builder had left without an order Emma had rung the estate agents who were handling the sale and had discovered that it would cost less to buy it than do the extensive amount of work that her own property would need.

With excitement mounting, she'd asked the estate agents if they would be interested in selling hers as well. If things worked out, she hoped she would be able to buy the house next to Glenn's, which was empty at present.

It would be heavenly to live in a place like that. She'd been unable to stop thinking about it for what was left of the weekend. But would she be able to sell her own monstrosity? And, more importantly, would Glenn want her as a neighbour?

'How did you find your father when you checked on him again yesterday?' was Emma's first comment when they met up on Monday morning in the passage outside their respective consulting rooms.

'Much better,' Glenn replied. 'And to prove it he was asking if you are still available to help with his Christmas Day event. My mother also wanted to know if you will be joining us as planned later in the evening.'

'The answer to both those questions is yes,' said Emma. 'I'm looking forward to both very much.'

'How did you fare with the builder?' he wanted to know, concealing the pleasure that her reply had given him. 'Did he go away with a big order?' When she shook her head Glenn asked in surprise, 'Why ever not? I thought you were all set for a big face-lift for your house?'

'His quote was too high,' Emma explained, 'and I've had a change of plan over the weekend.'

'Meaning what?'

'I've put my house up for sale and I'm going to buy the one next to yours if it is still on the market when I've sold mine.'

'I see,' he said in a monotone. 'And where has that idea originated from?'

'I've liked where you live from the word go, and something small but similar would be just right for my requirements.'

'And what if yours is still unsold when a buyer turns up for the one next to mine?' he asked in the same flat tone. 'What do you do then?'

'I'll worry about that when and if it happens,' Emma said, and called in her first patient of the day without further discussion.

CHAPTER SIX

EMMA'S FIRST PATIENT the next day was Anna Marsden, who had been in recently for her yearly checkup and was now back to have a chat about the results.

Newly retired from the position of manageress of Glenminster's largest womenswear boutique, Anna and her husband had been looking forward to a stress-free retirement. So Emma was not relishing having to let her know that the tests had shown that Anna had a type of blood clotting that showed signs of leukaemia and was going to need further investigation and treatment.

Anna's reaction to the news was typical of her. She listened to what Emma had to say and then responded calmly, 'Where do I go from here?'

'You have an appointment next Monday at the hospital,' Emma told her. 'Once you've chatted to the doctors there, you will have a clearer idea of what is involved.'

The woman seated across from her in the small consulting room smiled a twisted smile. 'Yes, of course, and at least I'll be able to have a lie-in when I feel like it now that I'm retired.'

When Anna left, the morning took its usual course of a steady flow of the sick and suffering coming and going. It gave Emma no time to question Glenn's reaction to the possibility that she might one day be living in the house next to his.

But in the lunch hour when Emma had a moment to spare and think about it properly, it became clear to her that although they'd spent some quality time together over the weekend he was still living in the past. There was no way she wanted to be in the background, chipping away at his love for the wife he had lost.

Yet it wasn't going to stop her from buying the house next to his if the opportunity presented itself. If Glenn was going to resent having her so near in his free time as well as being around constantly at the practice she would just have to accept the fact and get on with her life.

Glenn had just returned from visiting a patient who lived at the other end of the church graveyard from where the practice was. He popped in to inform her briefly that while there had been no sign of anyone hanging around the grave in the light of day, there had been fresh roses in one of the vases. Emma's niggling feeling of unease came flooding back.

With Christmas just a week away and her rash promise to spend some of the time with Glenn and his family hanging over her, Emma went to shop for the event on her way home that evening with little enthusiasm. She would be dining on one of the special nights of the year with people she hardly knew and could see it being an ordeal.

The daytime activity she'd volunteered for was different because she would be doing something useful in helping Glenn's father to bring some light into the darkness of other folks' lives. She wondered what his son would be doing while they were so employed. Putting up a fence between his house and the one next door?

Jonas had asked her if she could be at the community hall in the town centre for eight o'clock on the morning of Christmas Day as there were turkeys to be cooked in its spacious kitchens, along with all the other trappings. Within minutes of arriving Emma was at work along with a group of other volunteers who were mostly known to her from the practice, plus a couple of strangers. Glenn's father introduced her to one of them. His name was Alex Mowbray and he had lived in Glenminster many years ago before going to live abroad with his sick wife.

'I never wanted to leave this place,' Alex said, 'but my wife had a long-term serious illness. She wanted to move where it was warmer so I had no choice but to take her to live abroad.

'She died recently and my yearning to come back to Glenminster clocked in. So here I am, getting to know old friends who are still around and remembering with sadness those who are not.'

He seemed a decent sort, Emma thought as Alex Mowbray went back to his allotted task of preparing the vegetables that would be served with the turkey. Tall, with silver hair and kind blue eyes, he was easy to talk to, which was more than she could say for the man she was falling in love with. When she looked up, Glenn was there, having just arrived with a carload of provisions for the meal and an overwhelming urge to be near her.

So he wasn't going to be shut away in his castle for the day, like she'd expected, Emma thought joyfully. For at least part of the time he would be where she could see him.

Having unloaded the produce he'd brought, Glenn was beside Emma in a flash, smiling at the chef's hat she was wearing and asking if she was all set for the evening.

'Yes, if you still want me there,' she said. 'You didn't seem enthralled when I told you that I might be coming to live in the house next to yours.'

'That was merely the surprise,' he protested, 'and also because I don't take well to my secluded life being invaded.' It didn't seem like the moment to tell Emma that he wanted her living with him in his house, not in the small dwelling next to it.

Glenn looked around him. 'Dad is beckoning. He's going to tell me not to interfere with the workers. I'd better be off as I'm in charge of making sure that anyone unable to walk has transport to get here, which is going to involve half the practice staff making their cars available.'

'And I thought that you wouldn't be getting drawn into today's event,' she teased.

'What! With a father like mine?' He laughed and was gone again, leaving Emma to observe his father and Alex, who had appeared in their midst, chatting amicably as they performed their chosen tasks. Meanwhile Glenn and whoever was available from the practice staff were organising the transport that was going to be needed.

It was almost time for lunch and the kitchen staff were taking a short break before the diners arrived when Glenn's father informed Emma that he had invited their new acquaintance to dine with them that evening.

'Alex Mowbray lives alone,' he said, 'and that shouldn't happen to anyone at this time of year, so I've invited him to join us tonight.'

'Have you told your wife?' Emma teased, and he smiled.

'Yes, but she knows what I'm like. Olivia would be surprised if I *hadn't* invited someone else as well as you.'

'Is Glenn going to be happy, having me there?' she asked haltingly. 'I'm tuned in to how much he cherishes his privacy.'

'It has been difficult for him since he lost

Serena,' his father said, 'especially in such a dread-ful way. May I be allowed to say that since he brought you back to Glenminster out of nowhere, his mother and I have begun to hope.'

'I don't think you should if you don't mind me saying so,' Emma told him. 'We get on well most of the time, but the barriers that Glenn lives behind are not going to come down with me, I'm afraid.'

Glenn appeared at that moment with an elderly couple that he'd driven to the community hall and cast a quick glance at his father and Emma in a deep discussion that tailed off while he was finding seats for his passengers.

When Glenn had done that, he turned to go for his next lot of guests and found Emma beside him, smiling her pleasure at being near him again.

'So how many more journeys do you have to make?' she asked, and there was no smile in return.

'Just a couple,' Glenn replied, and then said, 'I hope that there's a table set for all the kind folk who have been doing the chauffeuring at my request.'

'Yes, of course,' she assured him, 'and tonight your parents will have another stranger at their table. Your father has also invited Alex Mowbray, who has re-cently returned from abroad after many years away.'

'Fine,' he said, and was off to pick up the last of the guests without giving her time to reply.

After the Christmas dinner was over, the guests had departed and the volunteers had tidied the place up, Emma began the short walk home. She hadn't wanted to take up a parking space, which would be in big demand, at the community hall so she'd walked there earlier. She could have waited for a lift from Glenn but along with the other car drivers he was busy taking guests home, while his father had gone to take the hall keys back.

Emma had only been on the way a matter of minutes when Alex's car pulled up beside her. Winding the window down, he asked, 'Can I give you a lift?'

'Er...yes, if it won't be out of your way, Mr Mowbray,' she said, deciding she'd like to get to know this amiable stranger better. 'I live just a short distance down the road.'

As she settled herself in the passenger seat next to him he said, 'So you'll know Waverly House, then?'

'Yes, I do,' she told him. 'It is a beautiful old property.'

'Yes, indeed,' Alex agreed. 'It was where my wife and I lived before we moved abroad and I have gained much comfort in finding it for sale and bringing it back to its former glory. Although sadly there will be no one for me to leave it to as we were never able to have children because of her health problems.'

What a charming man, Emma thought as she thanked him for the lift and went to prepare for the day's next big event. This time it would be Glenn who would be driving her to her destination and as she showered and dressed for the occasion the promise of the evening ahead was like a precious Christmas gift, probably the only one she was likely to receive.

But that didn't matter as long as Glenn liked what she had bought for him. She would never forget as long as she lived how he had painstakingly found her and persuaded her to come home. She could scarcely believe he was now the centre of her universe.

Glenn had said he would call for her at seven o'clock and as the clock climbed slowly towards that time every moment felt magical. Until it went past seven, then eight, and was teetering on nine. He must have had better things to do and had changed his mind about picking her up she thought dejectedly.

The phone rang at last and her heart skipped a beat when she heard Glenn's voice. 'I am so sorry, Emma,' he said contritely. 'I was involved in a pile-up as I was leaving the town centre.'

Her heart missed a beat. 'Are you hurt?' she gasped.

'No. I just had to help treat the casualties, who are now safely in A and E. I should be with you in minutes so don't run away.'

'Does your mother know?' Emma asked.

'Yes. She's been holding the meal back but is now ready to serve when we put in an appearance. I couldn't get in touch with you earlier as the accident occurred on the bottom road and I couldn't get a signal. We had to drive the casualties ourselves until we were higher up and then ambulances came speeding out to them. All the time I kept thinking that you would be judging me as yet another person letting you down. Tell me truthfully, did you?'

'Er...yes,' Emma said with painful honesty, 'because I know that in spite of our friendship you prefer to be alone, and I do understand that, Glenn.'

There was silence for a moment and then he said, 'I'll be with you in a matter of minutes—and be prepared. Dad is going to be wearing his Father Christmas outfit.'

As she watched for his car Emma felt ashamed for being so quick to judge him. She knew Glenn was decent and honourable and she loved him, she thought glumly. But the chances of her love being returned were not evenly balanced.

Glenn was as good as his word and his car pulled up outside within a matter of minutes. Emma saw immediately that what must have been a smart suit was ripped and bloodstained, but he was unharmed. In her relief at seeing that he wasn't hurt she leaned across the passenger seat and kissed his grimy cheek. 'Please, forgive me for doubting you,' she said softly.

'Of course,' Glenn said, reflecting that if he wasn't so scruffy and if his parents weren't patiently waiting for them to arrive, he might stop the car and show Emma how much she affected him. Within minutes they were pulling up outside his parents' house.

'Helping in an emergency such as tonight's is the

penalty of being a doctor,' Glenn said, as his mother held him close for a moment.

Alex nodded his agreement.

Glenn's father was helping Emma to take off her coat and when it was done he kissed her cheek lightly beneath the mistletoe and she felt tears prick her eyes.

They were a lovely family, she thought wistfully. What a shame that their daughter-in-law hadn't lived to give them grandchildren.

Glenn had disappeared in the direction of the bathroom and minutes later he appeared scrubbed and clean in casual clothes. They sat down to eat with a small gift from their hostess beside each plate, leaving Emma to wonder when she would get the chance to give Glenn what she had bought for him.

It came when the meal was over and the two of them were clearing away while the older folks relaxed after their exertions of the day in front of the sitting-room fire.

'I have something for you, Glenn,' she said awkwardly. He looked at her questioningly, and she said, 'Christmas seems an appropriate occasion to show my gratitude for all that you have done for me.' Taking a small gift-wrapped box out of her handbag, she offered it to him.

Glenn didn't accept it at first, leaving her standing with it in her hand. After a moment's silence he took it from her and said in a low voice, 'Whatever it is that you want to give me there is no need, Emma. What I did for you I would have done for anyone.'

'Yes. I know,' she said, feeling hurt that he had put her in her place. 'If you don't want to accept it, fine. The gift doesn't carry with it any commitments, just my grateful thanks.' She left him with the small package unopened in his hand and went to join the others, the question uppermost in her mind being how soon she could go home without causing offence.

When she'd gone back into the lounge Glenn groaned at his tactlessness. Why couldn't he have explained to Emma that he couldn't bear the thought of hurting her at some time or other by letting his dedication to Serena's memory come between them?

He had something for her that he was going to present in privacy tomorrow. He had already asked Emma out to lunch and he wanted to put his present where it belonged on her finger. But he knew that their relationship was not the usual kind and had no idea how she would react when she saw his gift.

When Glenn removed the wrappings and Emma's gift was revealed he swallowed hard. It was a gold pocket watch. He had admired a similar one belonging to a patient and Emma had remembered.

He opened the sitting-room door and when she looked up he beckoned to her. Unobserved by the others, who were engrossed in a carol service on television, she went to join him in the hall.

Taking her hand in his, he said softly, 'Your gift

is lovely, Emma. I am a tactless clod.' Pointing to the mistletoe sprig above their heads, he bent and kissed her long and lingeringly. He would have continued to do so if he hadn't heard movement coming from the sitting room because the programme they had been watching had come to an end.

Opening the door, Glenn smiled at them and said, 'Anyone for coffee?'

'Not for me, thanks,' Alex said. 'I came on foot and don't want to be too late getting back.'

'I'll be taking Emma home shortly,' Glenn said, 'and could drop you off after I've seen her safely home.'

Alex smiled. 'In that case, a coffee would be most acceptable.' And Emma thought, So much for the kiss. Apart from the time spent in the kitchen clearing up after the meal and the magical moments in the hall when Glenn had kissed her, they hadn't been alone for a moment all day. And now he was making sure they weren't by taking her home first.

There was the dry taste of anguish in her mouth, but pride stiffened her resolve and when Alex asked if that would be all right with her Emma flashed him a smile and said, 'Yes, of course.' And the matter was settled.

The fact that Glenn had spent no thought with regard to a Christmas gift for her was immaterial. Emma hadn't given him the watch expecting something in return. But it couldn't help bringing back that feeling of being of no importance, which had never gone away since the night Jeremy had told her she wasn't his and he wanted her gone.

They were outside her house and as she opened the car door and stepped onto the drive Glenn went round to her side and said in a low voice, 'It's late. I want to see you safely inside before I go. Emma, the reason I'm dropping you off first is because I want to know more about this stranger who has appeared out of nowhere. You have lived here a lot longer than I have, yet he isn't familiar to you, is he?'

'No, but Glenminster is a town, not a village where folks are much more likely to know each other,' she said. 'And from what Alex says, he has been long gone from here.' She glanced across to where he was waiting patiently for Glenn to get behind the steering-wheel again. 'All I know is that he seems a really nice man, and that he's rebought the house he used to live in and has refurbished it. It's a dream of a place.'

Emma instantly mellowed and, smiling at Glenn, said, 'I will be ready at twelve, as requested.' As the door closed behind her he got back into the car and drove off with his mind full of questions that had no answers.

When Glenn came for her the next day Emma was wearing the white fake-fur jacket and turquoise dress that she'd appeared in on that first night when everyone from the practice had welcomed her back to

Glenminster. His heartbeat quickened at the thought of what he was going to say to her over lunch.

'So what did you find out about Alex Mowbray?' she asked, when they were seated at the table that had been reserved for them in the Barrington Bar.

'Not a lot,' Glenn said. 'Except that he is a really nice guy who kept the faith with a sick wife but always wanted to come back here if the opportunity arose.'

'Do you know what was wrong with her?' asked Emma.

'Yes, advanced Parkinson's disease, which, as we both know, is an illness that doesn't carry with it an early death. The years must have crept by before he was able to come back to the place he loved best. But I didn't bring you here to talk about Alex,' he said with a change of subject. Now it was Glenn's turn to produce a small gift-wrapped box, which he put on the table in front of her.

'I know you must have thought me mean for not having a gift for you yesterday,' he explained, 'but I couldn't give you this then as what I have to ask you is private and very personal.' She sat watching him, transfixed by the moment, and he said, 'Maybe you would like to unwrap it to understand me better.'

'Yes, of course,' croaked Emma. She went weak at the knees when she saw that resting in a small velvet box was a solitaire diamond ring. It has happened at last, she thought joyfully. He wants me, he loves me. I can't believe it!

His next comment brought her back down to earth. 'I may never be able to be to you what you want me to be,' Glenn said gravely. 'To be totally committed I would have to give myself to you whole-heartedly, and I can't guarantee that I can do that by shutting Serena out of my life. So would you ac-cept second best? I care for you a lot, Emma, I re-ally do. And maybe one day I can be the way you want me to be.'

'No,' she breathed, and watched him flinch. 'I've had enough of being second best. I want to be with a man who will cherish me and who I can love in return, without making do with what is on offer. I only want your ring on my finger because you can't live without me and if that isn't so I will do without.'

Emma was getting to her feet and picking up her belongings, desperate to escape from the awful mo-ment of humiliation. When she'd collected her coat from the cloakroom she went into the foyer and flagged down a passing taxi to take her home, leav-ing Glenn to stare stonily at the ring she had cast aside.

Lying on top of the bed covers, gazing blankly up at the ceiling, Emma heard Glenn's car pull up in the drive below and turned her face into the pillows to deaden the sound of the doorbell when it rang. It continued for some minutes and then stopped, and she heard him drive off into the afternoon. When she went onto the landing and looked down into the hallway the box with the ring inside was lying on the doormat. It was then that the tears came as she went down slowly, picked it up, and without opening it again placed it in a nearby drawer.

When Glenn's father was driving past Glenn's house in the late afternoon he saw his son's car parked outside so stopped to have a chat. 'Where's Emma?' he asked in surprise. 'We thought that you weren't coming to us today because you had plans to spend it with her.'

'Yes, I did,' said Glenn, 'but it would seem that I presumed too much and she doesn't want my company.'

'I see,' Jonas replied, and asked disappointedly, 'What makes you think that?'

'I was a tactless fool, expecting too much of her,' Glenn replied bleakly, 'wanting what was best for me instead of her, and she refused.'

'Serena loved you,' his father said. 'Do you honestly think she would want you to cut yourself off from finding love again because she was taken?'

'Probably not,' Glenn agreed, 'but I still feel guilty because she wanted us to holiday somewhere else for a change, and I preferred to go to our usual place. She only went along with it to please me.'

'Yes, but you weren't to know that a tsunami was on its way that day,' Jonas protested.

'There is no answer to any of it,' Glenn replied.

'We've been through this discussion too often. I'll be fine here, getting some paperwork done, and will pop round for a bit later on if that's all right.'

'You know it is,' his father said. 'You've fed me often enough when your mother has had her fill of me. So we'll see you later, unless you've made friends with Emma again in the meantime.'

As if! Glenn thought bleakly. Emma brought out all his protective instincts one moment and the next stirred the heat of desire in him, and he wasn't getting any of it right.

When his father had gone Glenn left what he'd been doing and went for a brisk walk in the winter afternoon. He met Alex, doing the same thing. When he saw him Alex hailed him in his usual friendly manner and Glenn said, 'Are you looking forward to spending New Year in Glenminster?'

'You bet I am,' Alex said. 'I've wanted that for years. I was never able to come back to my roots until my wife passed away. I always had many precious memories of this place but it isn't the same as actually being here.'

'And I'm just the opposite,' Glenn told him. 'My memories are all in a faraway place and the last of them is not good.'

Having turned the screw on his heartstrings once again, Glenn went on his way with the thought that, like Alex, Emma was delighted to be back in their homeland, despite the gloomy nature of her return.

* * *

Unlike the two men, Emma was huddled beside the fire in her dismal sitting room with no inclination to move. The phone rang and Lydia's bright and cheerful voice came over the line.

'How are you fixed for coming to join me and mine for supper this evening?' she asked, and into the silence that followed she continued, 'I have visitors with me, relatives on holiday from Canada who have called unexpectedly, and I could do with some support.'

'Er...yes, I'm free tonight,' Emma told her reluctantly. 'What time do you want me there?'

'Seven o'clock, if that's all right,' Lydia replied.

'Yes, no problem,' she agreed, trying to sound enthusiastic.

When Lydia went on to say that she'd been trying to get in touch with Glenn to invite him round to give the occasion some support it was a relief for Emma to hear that she hadn't been able to contact him. The events of earlier in the day were still like a knife thrust in her heart.

Asked if she'd seen anything of Glenn, it hurt to admit that they'd met briefly at midday, but she had no idea what his plans were for the rest of it. With a sinking feeling inside she said goodbye to her friend and wondered where she was going to find the zest to socialise with Lydia's relatives.

CHAPTER SEVEN

WHEN GLENN RETURNED from his cheerless walk he found a message from Lydia awaiting him, and his reaction to it was the same as Emma's. The last thing he wanted to do was chat to strangers but Lydia was a tower of strength at the practice and a good friend so he didn't want to let her down.

The least he could do was help her to entertain her visitors and if Emma was there it would be a bonus. Even if she didn't want to have anything to do with him, just to be able to see her would help to lessen the nightmare he had managed to create for himself in the season of goodwill.

Emma was the first person Glenn saw when he arrived at Lydia's home. She was looking pale but composed with a wintry smile for him when he greeted her, which was in keeping with the weather outside and the misery he was experiencing inside being near her again.

What had she done with the ring? he wondered.

She'd put it with the rubbish in the waste bin most likely. Someone at the waste-disposal place might get a pleasant surprise, and if they did, good for them, as Glenn didn't want to see a reminder of his big mistake ever again.

He hoped and prayed that Emma wouldn't do a disappearing act again, as she'd done after Jeremy's hurtful treatment of her. He needed to be able to see her at the practice and around the place like he needed to breathe.

The Canadians were a pleasant lot, easy to get on with, and as the night progressed with a buffet that Lydia had arranged and lots of chatter Emma began to relax. At least the evening was proving to be a good opportunity for her to meet up with Glenn before seeing him at the practice when Christmas was over.

They had both walked the short distance to Lydia's house, thinking that driving wasn't a good idea if the wine was going to be flowing. At the first opportunity Glenn said to her in a low voice, 'No walking home alone, Emma. If you don't want me around, ring for a taxi.'

Emma nodded mutely as tiredness lay upon her like a heavy shawl after the day's events. There was no chance that she was going to opt for walking anywhere, she decided, and hoped that Lydia's guests might be feeling the same, having travelled quite some distance to see their hostess.

Yet it was midnight before the party was over and, doing as Glenn had suggested, Emma rang for a taxi. As it was the festive season there were long queues and it was going to be some time before her request was dealt with.

Glenn was observing her expression and guessed what the problem was. As they said goodbye to Lydia and her guests and went out into the night beneath a star-filled sky he said, 'You're going to have to let me walk you home, Emma.'

'I'll be fine on my own,' she told him flatly, and almost tripped over a tree root outside the house, but he caught her as she fell. As Glenn looked down at her in the circle of his arms he said, 'If you don't want me at your side on the way home I will be just a few paces behind you until you put the key in the door of your house. I will only leave you when you are safe inside. We still don't know the identity of the person who seems to have an endless supply of cream roses.'

As they set off, with Glenn walking a few paces behind, as promised, he said, 'There must have been other men in your mother's life, like the man who fathered you, for instance, and then disappeared.'

'If there were I never knew about them because I always thought that Jeremy was my father,' Emma said bleakly. 'And I had no reason to question it until that awful night when he put me straight and made me feel so unwanted.'

Glenn ached to hold her close, wanted to cradle

her to him instead of bringing up the rear, but after the dreadful mistake he'd made in showing Emma the ring and telling her she could only expect to be second best, hoping she could cope with that, he'd known that he had blown it with her. And rightly so, as far as she was concerned.

Glenn had said what he had because of the dread of not making Emma as happy, as she deserved, because in the dark corners of his mind there was always the memory of what had happened to Serena making him slow to make another commitment that he might fall down on. And yet it was Emma who was always the centre of his imaginings.

When they stopped at Emma's door she put the key in the lock and said meaningfully, 'You've seen me home safely, Glenn, and now my key is in the door.' She added, as it swung back on its hinges, 'So the only thing left to say is…goodnight!'

'Yes, all right, I get the message,' he said levelly. 'I just wanted to be honest with you, Emma, that's all.' He was striding off into the dark night when she called him back. When he turned round, Emma was standing holding the box, which she'd taken out of the drawer in the hall. 'You will need this when you find someone willing to accept second best,' she said tautly, giving it back to him. And as Glenn looked down at it bleakly, lying on the palm of his hand, the door was closed against him and Emma was walking slowly up the stairs to her lonely bed.

* * *

It was New Year's Eve and Emma was greeting the occasion with little enthusiasm. She had nothing planned and was intending to spend it alone in any case when the phone rang. It was Glenn's mother, to ask whether, if she wasn't booked to go anywhere, she would like to join them for supper as they welcomed in another year on the calendar.

When Olivia said that there would be just the three of them there—Jonas, Glenn and herself—the vision of Glenn insisting on her not going home alone came once again and she excused herself by pleading a headache and having an early night.

It didn't get her far. Olivia must have reported their conversation because minutes later Glenn was on the line, wanting to know if she had any medication for the headache, and if she didn't could he bring something round?

'I'll be fine,' she told him. 'I'm hugging a hot-water bottle and expect to be asleep in moments.' She knew that if he came round, and doctor that he was guessed that there was nothing wrong with her, it would be very hurtful for his parents. She liked them both a lot and didn't want to upset them.

'All right,' Glenn said. 'I don't expect you would have wanted to come in any case, but my parents aren't aware that we are not communicating so you will have to make allowances for them. They both set great store with the coming of a new year and are disappointed that you won't be there to share the moment with us. As far as the headache goes, if it starts to give you any problems I'll come round— *as a doctor, of course,*' was his parting comment, which left her feeling even more miserable.

Once the New Year was firmly established Emma didn't see much of anyone socially, except for Alex, who seemed to be the most agile out-and-about person amongst those who lived nearby. Emma had the feeling that the wanderer who had returned to Glenminster couldn't settle in his gracious house so she invited him round for coffee a couple of times.

Alex was an interesting person to talk to and she could imagine him being a loving father if ever he'd been blessed with children. Glenn would too, she mused ruefully. He had all the time in the world for the little ones who were brought to the practice by their parents with childish ailments.

Emma's closeness with Glenn had died after the business of the ill-fated proposal and although the days went by in a flash, the nights were long and lonely.

There had been a few viewers interested in her house. She had to show them round at weekends as her weekdays were swallowed up by the demands of her job. But she had received no offers for it so far. With the idea of living next door to Glenn no longer in her mind, she wasn't pushing for anything in particular yet she was still leaving her property on the market as daylight hours were becoming longer and

Easter was on the calendar. Soon those who sought a change of residence would be out and about.

Glenn observed her from a distance. At the practice Emma was still a dedicated doctor, putting her patients before anything else, but on the rare occasions when he saw her out of hours she had little to say and looked pale and remote. So much so that he wondered how long he could stand having to live with the evidence of how much he had hurt her.

Glenn cringed every time he thought back to his blundering proposal. It now seemed arrogant and hurtful, like a request for the best of both worlds. It also registered that she was seeing more of Alex Mowbray than him when she was away from the practice.

Yet Glenn was aware that sometimes young, insecure women often turned to older men for comfort and reassurance. Although the way that Emma had sent him packing didn't exactly indicate insecurity, more like outrage if anything.

The house next door to Glenn had been sold, but the board outside hers indicated no buyers as yet. Right now he would give anything for Emma to live near if he couldn't have her with him.

Flowers were still being placed on her mother's grave by an unknown hand and it seemed as if Emma was accepting the fact without further questioning. It was as if she was past caring. But Glenn wasn't prepared to let it rest at that. It was spooky and required an answer for Emma's sake, but short of him camping out in the churchyard it was almost as if the unknown visitor knew when to visit the grave and when not to.

And for Emma, who was all alone in the world—or at least didn't appear to have any other family—Glenn felt that if only he could bring a feeling of belonging into her life he would have done something to make up for his own lack of commitment.

Glenn was beginning to think of Serena less and Emma more but maybe that was because of the situation he found himself in: wanting Emma but afraid to give his heart to her completely and betray his love for his wife that he carried like a sacred torch.

There was one occasion when the flame of their attraction was ignited to fever pitch when Emma had driven to a hotel in the Gloucestershire hills to relieve the boredom of an empty weekend and Glenn was out walking with rucksack and walking boots for the same reason.

Easter would soon be upon them and with the awakening of plants and flowers and a pale sun above, the day had brought out those, like themselves, who loved the countryside.

Emma was about to order afternoon tea when his shadow fell across the table where she was seated out in the open, and he said gravely, 'Do you mind if I join you?'

'Er...no,' she said weakly, as the sight of him so near and unexpected made her blood warm and made her cheeks go pink.

A waitress was hovering to take their order and when that was done Glenn took the pack off his back and, facing her across the table, asked, 'So how are you, Emma? What brings you up here?'

She shrugged slender shoulders and told him, 'For the lack of anything else to do, I suppose. When the practice closed for the weekend at lunchtime I felt that I just had to get some fresh clean air after the long winter.'

'Me too,' Glenn agreed. 'Although I'm surprised not to find Alex with you. He told me once that he comes up here a lot to revive old memories, whatever they might be.'

'He's a lovely man,' she commented. 'But lonely, I feel. Alex once said that he came back because all his most precious memories are here. Whatever they might be, he was obviously happy in Glenminster, which is more than either of us can say, isn't it?'

As soon as she'd thrown that comment into the conversation Emma couldn't believe she'd said it. She'd given Glenn an opening for more aggravation and he was quick to respond.

'Which, I suppose, is my fault for being too faithful to the wife I lost?' he said, and got to his feet just as the waitress was bringing the food.

Emma felt the wetness of tears on her cheeks as he slung the bag he'd been carrying onto his back again and, leaving ample money on the table to pay for what they had ordered, set off back down the track on which he had come up.

She was on her feet, running after him. She caught up with him at the side of a deserted hayloft belonging to one of the farms. When Glenn turned to face her, Emma said breathlessly, 'Forgive me for my lack of understanding, Glenn, and for forgetting how you brought me back out of limbo. I will never forget that, no matter what.'

Her glance went to the hayloft, a close and sheltered place where they could be alone for a while. As if reading her mind, Glenn said, 'If ever I made love to you it would be on our wedding night, not in somewhere like that. Do you understand?'

'Yes, I do,' she said in a low voice. 'I understand perfectly and you have no idea how much it hurts to know how little chance there is of that.'

Glenn nodded and without speaking pointed himself homewards on the hillside, while she walked back to her car with dragging feet.

Following a miserable weekend that had seemed never-ending to Emma, they met again on Monday morning when she knocked on the door of his consulting room. After he opened it Emma said, before she choked on the words, 'I am sorry about what I said on Saturday, Glenn, and do hope you will forgive me.'

He reached out, took her hand in his, and pulled her into the room, closing the door behind her. 'There is nothing to forgive,' he said gently. 'I was too quick off the mark, Emma. But I have to tell

you that you would be better off with someone unlike me, whose heart and mind are free from pain
and sorrow.

'You are young and beautiful and deserve someone who isn't living in the past. It worries me that
you are so alone, without family, with just a few
friends. If we continue as we are doing one day you
will wish that you'd never met me, because all your
chances of happiness will be gone, lost in a relationship without roots, like your mother's was, from
what I can gather. Do you really have no idea at all
who your father was, or is? Have you ever seen your
birth certificate?'

'No,' she said. 'I've never had any need to look
for it, before now, and assumed Jeremy's name was
on it. But I can't find it anywhere, so maybe my real
father's name is included. I should get a copy and
see what comes to light.'

'Yes,' Glenn agreed. 'It can't do any harm. You
need to go to the register office where you were
born to apply for a copy. You will have to pay for it,
together with postage, on the spot. I'm told that it
doesn't take long to arrive.

'I'll come along to give you moral support if you
like and will be there for you when it arrives.' Then,
as the surgery doors were opened at that moment at
the start of another busy day, they separated, each
with a mind full of questions that needed answers.
And in the middle of it all Glenn prayed that the information Emma received from her birth certificate

would bring some degree of contentment into her life and help to take away the loneliness.

They went the next day in their lunch hour to the local register office to fill in the necessary paperwork for a copy of her birth certificate, and when they came out of the building Emma was smiling because, thanks to Glenn, hope had been born inside her. He pointed to a café across the road and said, 'How about a quick bite before we go back to the practice?'

'Yes, please,' she told him, and as they settled themselves at a table by the window Alex passed by on the other side of the street. He observed them and thought what a happy couple they made. He would have liked to go across and join them but didn't want to butt in and went on his way.

It was true. Emma had been happy on that day, just being with Glenn and knowing that soon one of the blank chapters of her life might be opened up to her. Her happiness lasted until the certificate she was waiting for arrived, with the information regarding her father described as 'unknown'.

It had been amongst her mail one morning and she had badly needed Glenn to hold onto for support. But he was missing from the practice that day, having to be present at the monthly meeting of senior medical staff in the town that was held in the board room of its biggest hospital. Without him the day seemed never-ending.

Glenn rang just as she was about to leave for home to see if she'd heard anything about her birth certificate. When she told him tearfully that she had, he told her to stay where she was at the practice, which was now empty as all the other staff had gone home. His meeting was over so he could be with her in minutes. Emma obeyed with the feeling that her life was keeping to its familiar pattern of emptiness.

When Glenn came striding in he held out his arms and Emma wept out her disappointment as he stroked her hair gently and asked, 'So what did it actually say?' As if he didn't know.

'It said "unknown",' she told him wearily, and as she looked up at him he bent and kissed her, gently at first and then with kisses that made her forget everything except that she was where she wanted to be.

When he released her from his hold and they locked up and went out into the dark street, it was as if the winter moon above was shining more brightly amongst a sky full of stars. Turning to her, Glenn asked softly, 'Shall we find somewhere to eat, Emma?'

'Yes,' she said, but when she looked up into his eyes she saw regret there and knew he was wishing they could be back to the way they had been before, which was not on kissing terms. Although there had been no lack of tenderness and desire while she'd been in his arms.

There was a restaurant not far away and Glenn steered her towards it, devastated that the thing that Emma so much needed to know hadn't been forthcoming. He was also cross with himself for allowing her to hope for something again.

'Would you like to stay at my place tonight?' he asked when they left the restaurant. 'I don't like to think of you all alone with such a disappointment to cope with.'

The offer was tempting, but there was no way that she wanted to be so close to him yet out of bounds, so reluctantly she said with a catch in her voice, 'Thanks for the offer, Glenn, but I'll be fine. I might do some searching around the house to see if there is anything that might guide me to who my father was. I doubt it, though, because the last thing that Jeremy said after taking the ground from under my feet was that my mother had never told him the name of the man who had made her pregnant. So I don't see her leaving any names or addresses around, do you?'

Glenn sighed. 'No, not really, I suppose, and are we really saying that she married Jeremy and put up with him for twenty-plus years so you would have a father?'

'Yes, it seems to have been that way,' said Emma sadly, 'and I never knew anything different until Jeremy enlightened me.'

'What did your mother die from, Emma?'

'She was frail, probably from unhappiness that she never let me see, and had a heart problem that culminated in a sudden serious heart attack one day. She was rushed to hospital but it was too late to save her, which left Jeremy and me to jog along as best we could with nothing at all in common.'

They had parked their cars not far from the place where they'd gone to order the birth certificate, and Glenn was only sorry that it had proved fruitless. There was nothing more to say, it was time to say goodbye, but he wasn't willing to give up on it. He said, 'If you don't want to stay at my place, shall I stay with you at yours?'

She flashed him a tired smile. 'No, I'll be fine. Don't worry about me.'

'All right,' he agreed. He couldn't blame her if she wanted to hold him at bay, but he still couldn't help feeling concerned. 'I'll go, but only if you promise that you will ring me if you need me at any time during the night, and that you will come to me for breakfast before we start at the practice. Otherwise I will come to your place to fetch you. Right? Understood?'

'Yes,' she replied. Despite her anxieties about their relationship, his concern on her behalf felt like healing balm. Feeling better, she drove off into the night.

Glenn stopped off at his parents' house on the way home and asked if either of them knew of anyone who might have had an affair with Emma's mother before she'd married Jeremy Chalmers.

They both looked at him blankly, and Jonas said, 'No, we don't. Emma's mum was local, while Jeremy came from somewhere near where she'd worked before Emma was born. Emma was just a toddler when he came as head of the practice.'

And his mother chipped in with, 'Why do you want to know something like that?'

'It was just that I was curious,' he told her, 'because Emma tells me that she and Jeremy weren't at all close.'

Olivia laughed. 'So aren't you the lucky one to have people like us as your parents?'

'I certainly am,' he replied, holding her close, while his father's comment was to the effect of when was he going to give them some grandchildren? At other times the question had irritated him because of his devotion to Serena's memory, but this time it had its appeal as suddenly the thought of having a little girl or boy who looked like Emma was firing his imagination.

When Emma appeared at his door the next morning, geared up for the coming day amongst the sick folk of Glenminster, Glenn breathed a sigh of relief.

He hadn't slept well at all because he'd kept imagining her being sad and lonely in the night hours and now, observing Emma, she looked the more rested of the two of them.

Glenn had gone to the trouble of making a cooked breakfast with all the trimmings, which was the last thing he would ever normally contemplate on a working day. When she saw what was on offer Emma said, 'Glenn, this is delightful. I will enjoy every mouthful.' How great it would be if they could have breakfast together every day after sleeping in the same bed, she thought. Her colour rose at the idea, and then their glances held. He smiled across at her and said, 'We must do this again some time.'

'Yes,' she said, glowing at the thought, 'that would be lovely.' And suddenly the misery of the previous day seemed far away. That was until they got to work and Lydia told them that on arriving at the practice she had seen an abundance of fresh flowers on the grave. And the same question about who the mysterious person who had known her mother could possibly be haunted Emma once more.

Glenn was close behind her and as he watched the colour fade from her face the determination within him to solve the mystery once and for all hardened. Anything to take away the hurt Emma felt every time it happened, even if he had to stay up all night.

There had to be a reason why the flowers were always cream roses, especially when golden daffodils and hyacinths were in bloom and there was cherry blossom on the trees. These roses were hothouse-grown, and if they were chosen for a special reason Emma had no knowledge of it.

Observing the number of blooms that had been put there only minutes ago it seemed logical to expect that it would be some time before the phantom mourner came again. When he or she did Glenn was determined he was going to be ready.

'Who can it possibly be, Glenn?' Emma said as they went inside the practice together. 'I know all my mother's friends and none of them frequent the graveyard or relieve the florists of most of their stock in one go.'

'I don't know,' Glenn said grimly, 'but I'm going to find out, and when I do they will have some explaining to do.' His voice softened. 'You don't deserve this, Emma. I want you to be happy and carefree.' She stared at him doubtfully, and he added, 'Yes, I know I haven't been helping that along much, but I have the matter in hand.'

It was only as they separated, each to their own consulting room, that Emma wondered what that meant.

It was half-term and quite a few parents were there with their young ones for various reasons. As ever on days like this the sound of young voices and small feet came from the play area of the practice, put there to keep the young patients happy until their names were called.

There was also the sound of fretful crying from one little one who had just arrived with worried parents. Glenn must have heard it as he came out of his consulting room as the patient he'd just seen was leaving and told them to take their little girl inside immediately.

Not long after he came out and told Reception in a low voice, 'We need an ambulance fast.' He turned to Emma, who was nearby and had heard the little one's crying. 'I suspect meningitis. The dreaded red rash is there and the other symptoms also make it look likely.'

His comments brought a sudden hush amongst those who were near enough to have heard what he'd said. After the ambulance had been and gone, with siren blaring as it sped on its way, a sombre silence hung over those who were still waiting to be seen.

After the dreadful beginning the day settled into a more normal routine and as the ills of winter became the main topic of conversation in the waiting room someone who had been absent for a while turned up in the form of James Prentice. He had been on a two-month course up north in a hospital there and was back with a new girlfriend in tow and expecting everyone to be as bowled over by her as he was.

With just a momentary lull following his arrival and a few quick handshakes for the new woman in his life because everyone was so busy, James left after announcing that they were getting engaged and would be in the Barrington Bar that evening if anyone would like to join them for a drink.

'That would seem to be a whirlwind romance,' Glenn said whimsically, as he and Emma were about to leave the practice at the end of what had been a very busy day. 'Are you intending to go to this evening's get-together? I shall go for a while to represent the practice but won't be staying long as I've got paperwork to deal with. I never seem to have the time to get to it during the day. So I can give you a lift there but can't promise to be able to bring you back.'

'Thanks for the offer,' she told him. 'I would appreciate it as my car is due for servicing. I can get a taxi to take me home if you've gone when I'm ready to leave. So what time will you pick me up?'

'Is seven o'clock all right?'

'Er...yes,' she replied absently with her mind elsewhere. 'Have we any report yet on the little girl with suspected meningitis?'

'It came through just a few moments ago,' Glenn said. 'She does have it, but they are hopeful that it was caught in time, so she should avoid any serious complications and she'll recover.'

'Poor little one,' Emma said sadly. 'I hate to hear of a child suffering.'

'I'm afraid that goes with the job,' Glenn said, 'but there is the other side to what we do for sick children—we make them well again in most cases because of our treatment and care.' Suddenly feeling that he was walking on eggshells, he said, 'Do you ever want children, Emma?'

She swivelled to face him. 'Yes, of course,' she said immediately. 'To have someone that I belong to and who belongs to me would be a dream come true. But I can't produce them without some assistance, I'm afraid.'

'Were you and Serena planning on having a family?' she asked with a casual sort of interest that was meant to preclude any kind of offence.

He took her breath away with his response.

'Yes, we wanted children,' Glenn told her, 'and we'd already done something towards that end. Serena was four months pregnant when that tsunami came out of nowhere. Mine was a double loss, so can you blame me for doing nothing about it when my parents bemoan their lack of grandchildren? I never told them about the pregnancy. I felt they had enough to cope with with the loss of their daughter-in-law.'

Emma's eyes were big and tears hung on her lashes as she turned to face him, stunned to hear that Glenn had been carrying around an even bigger burden than she'd known. Reaching out, she stroked the hard line of his jaw tenderly and with a groan he pulled her into his arms and held her close. And in that moment Emma knew that if he should never want her to be permanently in his life she would abide by it. That there would never be any other man that she would love as she loved him.

CHAPTER EIGHT

WHEN GLENN CALLED for her, as promised, at seven o'clock Emma was ready but showing little enthusiasm for the unexpected get-together that James had arranged. Observing her expression, he said wryly, 'Something tells me that we're not going to be the life and soul of the party tonight.

'I'm sorry, Emma, I would never have told you about the baby if the subject hadn't come up, and I don't want it to put a blight on your life too. I've learned to live with it. In these kinds of situations one has no choice. At least there's one bright side to tonight's event.'

'And what's that?' she questioned.

'Now he's engaged, Prentice will stop hanging around you. One day the right man will come along and you will find the happiness that you deserve.'

'Don't preach to me, Glenn,' Emma said tightly. 'You've made it clear that I'm not part of your agenda. And as I've already had the unpleasant experience of being told I wasn't wanted by my stepfather, the two together are enough to make me shy away from any future relationships on a permanent basis.'

'Wow! What did I do to deserve that?' he asked, swivelling to face her. 'I was merely referring to the many surprises that life always has in store and thinking how much Jeremy hurt you. I don't want to follow it with something similar.'

When there was no reply forthcoming, he asked, 'So, are you coming or not? Like I said, I'm going but not for long, and the night will be gone if we don't make a move.'

'Yes, I'm coming,' Emma told him, not willing to miss spending some time with Glenn regardless of what she'd said before. So soon they were amongst the rest of the staff, drinking champagne and toasting the newly betrothed couple with smiles that gave no hint of any inward turmoil.

An hour later, when Glenn said reluctantly that he was ready for the off and reminded her to travel home by taxi, with no detours near the church, he added, 'I am determined to find this mysterious person who puts the flowers on your mother's grave so frequently. In the meantime, Emma, don't let it upset you.

'You'll be the first to know when I solve the mystery and I think you will feel better if you keep away from it for a while.'

Emma nodded, ashamed of her earlier outburst, and with that, Glenn was gone.

As he drove the short distance home Glenn was remembering what he'd said to Emma about the grave. It was true that so far he was clueless, and a graveyard wasn't the best place to hang out, but he had to sort it out for her sake.

He felt sure he was missing something that was staring him in the face. And somehow it had to be connected with Emma—but what? Was it from her past, or her mother's? And if it was, how did he unravel the mystery? There must still be people around in Glenminster who had known Emma's mother and who she was seeing before she fell pregnant.

What about his parents, for instance? He'd already tried to sound them out, to no avail. But they'd lived in Glenminster as long as he could remember and his father had always socialised a lot. Maybe he should have another go at sounding him out and seeing if he came up with anything of interest? Mind you, knowing his dad, Jonas would have said if there was anything that he, Glenn, ought to know in connection with his friendship with Emma. Besides, his parents didn't know about the cream roses that graced the grave so regularly.

When he arrived home Glenn put the problem to the back of his mind while he attended to the demands of the practice. But once that was done it was there again, the niggling worry that there might be something that was going to cause Emma pain one day if he didn't pin it down for her.

From the size of the floral display it could be

two to three weeks before the next visit from the mystery mourner. Whoever it was must have had a great deal of regard for the woman buried there, and would surely come back. Hopefully, by then he might have a plan ready that would bring the person into the open.

In the meantime, there was a severe cough doing the rounds that had some of the patients barking in the waiting room, and amongst the elderly, who were only just warming up after winter's chill, there were cases of bronchitis, while for the rest there was a virus here and there, and always a full list.

But during each busy day Glenn could rely on Emma and the practice team with their skills and dedication to their professions. He was more content than he had been for a long time, until the cream roses began to droop and he knew the time was approaching when he might come face to face with the person who might somehow be connected with Emma. He really hoped he could come up with a solution to the problem.

But would Emma want to meet the person who must have known her mother so well that they brought flowers so often and in such a secretive manner? Would he if it were him? Whoever it was, they had given Emma no means of discovering his or her identity.

Having no wish to spend twenty-four hours of every day in the churchyard, Glenn had changed his consulting room with that of one of the other doctors because it overlooked the grave in question. He'd also asked the vicar to keep an eye open for anyone bringing flowers to it around the time he thought they were due.

But as the days went by no one went anywhere near the grave for any reason whatsoever. The only folks around seemed to be just local people taking the same short cut that he did when he went to visit his elderly patient on the road that led past the church. In the end Glenn had to accept that maybe the strange behaviour of the person he sought had just been a joke or a fad, and that there was no cause for concern on his part.

As the time continued to pass uneventfully Glenn had to tell Emma when she asked that so far it seemed that either the person knew they were being watched and had given up the practice of leaving flowers on the grave, had gone to live elsewhere, or it had been some kind of a long-term mistake. Emma had accepted his comments at face value but deep down wanted an answer, a name to set her mind at rest.

The first thing Glenn did on arriving at the practice the morning after that conversation was to go into the churchyard to inspect the grave. He was relieved to find it still empty of fresh blooms, but by lunchtime they were there again. He thought that, short of keeping watch out in the cold all the time, the mystery could go on for ever and he had patients

ABIGAIL GORDON   155

already arriving who needed his time much more than a display of cream roses.

Emma had seen Glenn go across and when he came back could tell from his expression that the flower person had returned from wherever they had been. Observing how much it upset her, Glenn knew that he couldn't proceed with his plans for the Easter weekend if it meant leaving her behind in that sort of a situation.

With Easter approaching had come light and brightness after winter's dark days. Before the mystery flowers had reappeared Emma's spirits had been lifted for quite some time, while Glenn had been considering doing what he always did at Easter.

The practice would be closed for the long weekend and he had intended following his usual routine and spending the time in Italy, where he was in the habit of renting a house on the Amalfi coast that belonged to a friend from his college days.

He always found the change of scene therapeutic and restful, but this time he felt that he couldn't relax knowing that he would be leaving Emma behind to cope with her dark moments and that he was responsible for some of them.

As the time drew nearer he wondered what sort of a reception he would get if he invited her to join him for the Easter break purely as a friend, putting aside all other thoughts and just enjoying themselves in the magic of Italy.

Knowing that he wouldn't rest until he'd asked

her, Glenn waited until they were the first arrivals at the practice one morning and asked if she had a moment to spare.

'Well, yes,' Emma said laughingly, as her glance went around the empty waiting room and on the forecourt outside, and he wondered how long her light-heartedness would last when she heard what he had to say.

It seemed as if he had reason to worry as Emma's smile had disappeared within seconds and she was shaking her head. 'I don't think so,' she said in a low voice. 'That part of Italy is incredibly romantic and beautiful and I would love to go there, Glenn, but feel that it would be more sensible to stay at home. Thank you for inviting me and I hope you have a lovely time.'

He gave a twisted smile and, not wanting to give up easily, said, 'Do you think either of us will have a "lovely time" in one of the world's most beautiful places if we are on our own?'

'No, I suppose not,' she agreed weakly, and decided that it was only four days in Italy they were discussing, not a lifetime. And it *would* be a relief to be away from the mystery of the never-ending flowers on the grave.

'When would we fly out if I came?' Emma asked doubtfully.

'Thursday night, so as to be already there for Good Friday,' Glenn replied, and hoped that she was weakening.

The house had four bedrooms so Emma could have her choice, and there was no likelihood of him being missing when she woke up as when he was there he was always on the patio, soaking up the sun, at an early hour.

'So do I book you a flight for Thursday night or not?' Glenn asked patiently, as the practice began to come alive with the sound of voices inside and out.

'Er...yes...I suppose so,' Emma said. 'It would be a brief change of scene and I need something like that.' And before he could comment further she went to where her first patient of the day was waiting.

So much for enthusiasm, he thought, but at least she'd said yes.

Enthusiasm was more in evidence when Glenn called to pick her up on the Thursday night to go to the airport. There was a smile for him and as he observed Emma's outfit of leggings with a smart silk shirt above them and her weekend case, waiting to go into the boot of his car, his spirits lifted.

They chatted easily enough during the flight and he hid a smile at Emma's expression when she saw the house. It was a very attractive residence, overlooking the sea, and moonlight was shining on the water. It was already quite late after their evening flight.

'There are four bedrooms,' Glenn told her. 'Choose whichever one you want. There's a chef who lives nearby who comes in to do the food, so for a short time we shall be living in style. I've got a hire car due to arrive tomorrow, so shall we drive along the beautiful Amalfi coast? Or do you want to just laze about as we've got here so late?'

'It all sounds fantastic,' Emma said. 'I was crazy not to want to come, but nothing seems right in my life any more except my job at the practice. I am totally content with that. But the mystery of the flowers gets me down and…'

'Go on, say it,' Glenn told her. 'You don't get much joy out of me either. I know what you thought about my proposal. I must have been out of my mind to be so patronising. I hope that one day you can forgive me, Emma.'

'I think I already have,' Emma replied. 'It was wrong of me on that occasion not to take into account the memory of how Serena died and how difficult that must be to live with all the time.'

Glenn was smiling. 'So shall we put all our sad thoughts to one side and enjoy our time together for the next few days?'

'Yes, why not?' Emma agreed, and kissing him lightly on the cheek went slowly up the stairs to the bedroom she had chosen, content to know that Glenn would be near while she slept. Anything further than that would happen only if they both wanted it to, and finally it seemed as if that might be the case.

The following morning they swam in the pool and lay in the sun and the day dawdled along contentedly with every glance, every touch a promise. When it was time to go up to change for the evening meal Glenn bypassed his room and followed Emma into hers. He slipped the towelling robe that she'd been wearing by the pool off her shoulders and kissed every part of her that wasn't covered by her swim-suit until she was melting at his touch. It was like coming in out of the wilderness to happiness and joy.

But the telephone on the bedside table had other ideas and when Glenn released her to answer its strident ring Emma saw his expression change. Her heart missed a beat as he said, 'We'll get the first flight out and go straight to the hospital.' As he re-placed the receiver he said grimly, 'That was my mother. Dad climbed a tall tree in the garden this afternoon to rescue their cat, which had gone up it to escape next door's dog. When it wouldn't come down he stretched an inch too far to reach it, over-balanced and fell down onto the stone path below.'

'And?' Emma questioned anxiously.

'He's in hospital with a fractured arm and leg and my mother needs me, I'm afraid.'

'Yes, of course,' Emma agreed immediately, with a vision of his energetic father hurt and fretful. 'I'll tell the chef that we have to leave while you book a flight.'

'So much for our special time together,' Glenn said flatly. 'I was going to suggest that we go along the Amalfi coast tomorrow. Do you think it wasn't meant to be?'

'No, of course not,' Emma told him gently. 'At present your parents have to come first.'

'Yes, of course,' he agreed, 'but it is typical of Dad that he thinks he can shin up a tree at his age without getting stuck. He sees himself as Superman, thinks that he's invincible. Apparently while he was lying at the bottom of it the cat came down of its own accord without any trouble and ran off.'

They found Jonas sitting up in bed, looking bruised and crestfallen to have been the cause of them having to fly home so soon. Emma told him gently that there was no blame attached to what he had done, and said to Glenn that he was lucky to have a father to love and cherish him. In the silence that followed there was no one amongst them who wanted to contradict that.

A nurse was hovering with the comment that the patient needed some rest and would be in a better condition for chatting the following day, and as they prepared to leave, Jonas said to Glenn, 'Be sure to come tomorrow. We need to talk, and it will give your mother a chance to rest.'

'Yes, sure,' he agreed, 'and in the meantime don't go climbing any more trees.'

'You might be thanking me for climbing that tree soon,' was the reply, and they left the patient in the care of the nurse and took Glenn's mother home to rest.

'I didn't want to bring you back from your break,' Olivia said, 'but Jonas insisted and made such a fuss he was causing alarm amongst the nursing staff.' She turned to Emma. 'You must think us a strange family, my dear.'

'As someone who hasn't got one, I envy you more than words can say,' she replied, and felt like weeping.

'I want you to stay at my place tonight,' Glenn told Emma as they drove the short distance to his house after seeing his mother safely settled. 'Not for any other reason than I want you to be where I know you are near. It has been a strange day. Only hours ago we were in Italy and then we got that phone call. Did you think Dad was OK when we got there? He seemed strange, don't you think?'

'Yes,' Emma agreed. 'It was as if he knew something that we weren't aware of, unless he was suffering from concussion.'

'We'll have to see what tomorrow brings,' Glenn said. 'Are you hungry? We haven't eaten in ages.'

'Just coffee and a biscuit will suit me fine,' Emma said softly. 'Thank goodness that it's Saturday tomorrow.'

'I couldn't agree more,' Glenn said, and added, 'The guest room is ready, just help yourself to anything you find there. I'll bring your case up so that you have your own nightwear available if you would prefer it. Emma, there won't be any locked doors between us.'

'Good,' she said. 'So if I'm up first am I allowed to bring you a cup of tea?'

'Yes, of course, but I haven't brought you here to wait on me. I just want you where you are safe and free from care, and I never feel that you are either of those things in that house of yours.'

'I can't do anything about that until I find a buyer,' Emma said, 'and I'm sure you will agree that it isn't the usual "desirable residence" that the average house hunter is seeking.'

She was asleep within moments of settling into Glenn's guest room this time and when she awoke the next morning, with a bright sun shining up above, the memories of the day before came back— the delights of Amalfi and Capri that hadn't mate- rialised, the moment when Glenn had caressed her and held her close, only to have it taken from them by the news of his father's fall from the tree that had caused their hasty return to Glenminster.

What would today bring? Emma wondered. Some degree of recovery for Glenn's father hopefully, but he was elderly and a fall of that severity could have serious after-effects.

When she went down to breakfast, having show- ered and changed into fresh casual clothes, Glenn was on to the hospital, asking when it would be con- venient to visit his father who, it seemed, had been restless in the night and impatient to see his son.

'Shall I drop you off at your place on my way to

the hospital when we've had breakfast?' Glenn suggested, after assuring the hospital that he would be
there as soon as possible.

'Yes, that would suit me fine,' Emma told him. 'It
would give you some private time with your family
and I can check the post and get in touch with the
estate agent to see if there have been any viewings
of the house while I've been away. Before we separate, would you like to come there for a meal this
evening? It's time that I offered you some hospitality for a change.'

Glenn hesitated for a second and then said, 'That
would be great, Emma, but I'm not sure what the day
is going to bring with regard to my father. Can we
put that on hold for the time being?'

'Yes, of course,' she agreed, with the feeling that
maybe Glenn was relieved that their closeness of the
last couple of days was being slowed down by unexpected circumstances. And she was back to her
feeling of aloneness, knowing that he was the only
person who could change that.

There was no mail when Emma arrived back at
the house, which was not surprising considering the
short time she'd been away, but a phone message
from the estate agent was waiting to the effect that
there had been a viewer in her absence who might
be interested in her property, but instead of feeling
uplifted at the thought, Emma's feeling of being sur-
plus to requirements gained momentum.

* * *

When Glenn arrived at the hospital two things were obvious. The first was that his father was in full control of all his faculties, and the second was his eagerness to pass on to his son the reason why he had actually fallen from the tree, which in the first instance sounded less believable than Glenn could have imagined.

'I fell because Pusscat had taken herself high up onto one of the branches to get away from next door's dog,' Jonas explained, 'and as I was reaching for her and in full control of the situation I glimpsed someone going past on the pavement across the way, carrying a large bunch of cream roses. And as I stretched myself further along the branch to get a better look, it gave way.'

'So you didn't see who it was, which gender?' Glenn asked.

'No. All I saw after that was stars as I hit the ground.'

'Did you manage to see what this person was wearing?'

'Only a glimpse before I lost my balance. It seemed like a long grey belted raincoat with a pull-down hat as it was raining at the time, and then I was falling.' Jonas was nearly back to his usual self. 'But I shall expect to be referred to as Sherlock in any future confrontations.'

'You're amazing,' Glenn told him gently, 'to risk life and limb like that for Emma's sake.'

'Aye, maybe,' he replied, 'but I didn't find out who the cream roses were from, did I?'

'Not yet, but it's a lead that we can follow.'

The nurse that Glenn had spoken to on the phone was near and she said gently, 'It is time to rest now that you have seen your son, Mr Bartlett. The doctor is on his way to see how you are this morning and we don't want you tired or overexcited, do we?'

'You're not going to raise any false hopes for Emma, are you?' was his father's last comment as Glenn prepared to leave.

'No, not until I have the right answer,' Glenn replied, and added as he left, 'And now do as the nurse says, Dad, and get some rest.'

On the way home, Glenn stopped off at the church to check if flowers had been recently placed on the grave, and sure enough they were there. But who had brought them and why was something he had yet to discover.

The wording on the gravestone referred to Emma's mother's maiden name, rather than her married one, which was strange. It had a sound of Jeremy about it, and meant that anyone knowing Helena from the distant past would have no knowledge that Emma was her daughter.

It was not surprising that Emma hadn't known about her real father until Jeremy had told her the truth so brutally and she had fled Glenminster until he had tracked her down and brought her home.

On his way home Glenn called to see Emma to

make sure she was all right after he had left her so abruptly to visit his father, but there was no answer when he rang the doorbell. As midday was approaching he stopped off at one of the places where they had lunched a couple of times in the hope that she might be there.

But it was not to be, and despite his efforts he couldn't find her. So once he had eaten he went to report the patient's progress to his mother, who had been having a quiet morning knowing that he would have seen his father. She was preparing to go in later for the afternoon visiting.

'Where's Emma?' she wanted to know. 'I was so sorry to have dragged you both away from the delights of Italy after such a short stay.'

'I would have been sorry if you hadn't,' he told her, 'and so would Emma. She is somewhere around but I'm not sure where. I've just called at her place but she wasn't there. She stayed at my house last night as I didn't want her going back to that dismal place of hers after Italy.'

Emma was in the town centre at the offices of the estate agent, following up the message that she'd received about an interested viewer of her house. When she got there she discovered that they had seen the house a second time that morning and had made an offer.

'Really?' she exclaimed. 'I can hardly believe it.'

The estate agent explained that the house was big

and well built even if it wasn't exactly the last word in design, which had helped it to sell. He asked if she was going to accept the offer.

'Yes, please,' she said. The thought uppermost in her mind was that with money in the bank she would be free to go where she wanted. And if Glenn continued to keep her at a distance, she could start again somewhere new, where there was no pain or longing.

CHAPTER NINE

EMMA RANG GLENN that evening and the lift in her voice said she had good news of some sort to impart.

'I've got a buyer for the house,' she told him, and there was silence for a moment.

'Wow!' he exclaimed. 'Fast work! Well done! And where are you planning to move to?'

Your house, with you, Emma would have liked to say, but it would seem that thought hadn't occurred to him, or surely he would have suggested it?

'I have no idea at the moment,' she replied. 'I only learned this afternoon that I had a buyer.'

'Yes, of course,' Glenn said. 'Why don't I come round and take you to dine somewhere nice to celebrate the occasion? Would you like that, Emma?'

Would she like it? Of course she would! 'Yes, that would be nice,' Emma said. 'I'll need some time to get ready, though.'

'How long?'

'An hour or so. But what about your father, Glenn? Oughtn't we to go to evening visiting instead?'

'We'll go to the hospital first and dine afterwards, if that is all right with you.'

'Yes, I'd love to do that. Your family are amazing,' Emma said. 'I do so envy you, Glenn.'

He wanted to tell Emma about the person in the grey raincoat carrying the flowers, but he was worried that it might spoil their evening. There would be time enough to tell her when he'd eventually found the identity of the mystery donator.

Emma had dressed with care in a wraparound cream silk dress that enhanced the dark attraction of her hair and eyes, and with complementary jewellery to match and shoes that brought her almost level with Glenn's height. She surveyed herself before answering his ring on the doorbell. She thought she must be crazy to think there was anything other than mild interest from Glenn. Ever since they'd had to leave Italy he had seemed withdrawn. And yet she still felt compelled to dress with care. Yes, she really must be crazy.

Her efforts, it seemed, did not go unnoticed. When Glenn saw her, there was longing in his glance, tenderness around his mouth and hope was born in her again, briefly. But it faded when he commented that, it being a mild evening, she might not need the jacket she'd brought with her. And in the car as they drove to the hospital there was no closeness, just the same small talk.

* * *

Jonas shot Glenn a questioning look when they appeared and when his son shook his head, the patient tutted his impatience. He reached for a fruit drink that was standing on the locker next to his bed, and as Emma chatted with Olivia, who had come back for evening visiting, Glenn whispered, 'I'm working on it, Dad. Woe betide anyone wearing a grey raincoat who comes into my line of vision! But it might have to wait until we have another shower. It could be a garment that only comes out in wet weather. And there's also the fact that it might just be a co-incidence. You could have seen someone with the same kind of flowers.'

'Yes, I know,' Jonas said, 'and I'm fidgety. I want to be out of this place to help you find this person, but the doctor says not yet.'

'A rest for once will do you no harm,' Glenn told him, 'and I'll be in touch the moment I have any news, all right?'

'Yes. Now, go and enjoy your evening and perhaps you could drop your mother off on the way to wherever you are going.'

'Of course,' Glenn said, and thought how fortunate he was to have both of his parents still fit and well, apart from his father's injuries. Thankfully the fall from the tree hadn't done too much damage and he was responding satisfactorily to treatment. If only there was a family like his for Emma, where she could feel loved and wanted.

He could give Emma one that was theirs alone if she would only let him, but she needed to know where she came from before that and just who it was who was so interested in her mother's grave.

Glenn had booked a table at a restaurant on one of the tasteful shopping promenades that Glenminster was famed for and as they waited to be served, he said, 'So tell me what your mother was like, Emma. Do you resemble her at all?'

'No, not in any way,' she said. 'Mum was blonde with blue eyes, while my hair is dark and my eyes are hazel. We were of a similar build but that's the only resemblance. Why do you ask?'

'Just curiosity, that's all,' Glenn said easily. 'What sort of a job did she have before she had you?'

'She was secretary to the manager of one of the big banks in Glenminster, but had to give it up when I was born. Jeremy told me on the night I left that she had only married him to gain respectability and to give me a father.'

'And did you believe him?'

'It might have been true in one way, but she certainly paid the price for it. He ruled the roost and was prone to remind her frequently how much she was indebted to him, which I didn't understand at the time because I had no reason to think that he wasn't my father.'

'So you really have no idea who your birth father could be? No special friends of your mother's?'

'No, I'm afraid not,' Emma said regretfully. 'I remember when I was small my mother cried a lot. As I grew older we were very close, like sisters almost, but she never breathed a word. And after she died I jogged along with Jeremy's fads and fancies, having no idea that he wasn't my father. Until, as I told you, he wanted to remarry, told me to go, and when I protested, put me well and truly in the picture with such devastating results.'

'The low-life!' he gritted. 'But why didn't he remarry?'

'It was Lydia that he wanted to marry, but as soon as she realised how he had treated me she called it off.'

The food they had ordered was being placed in front of them and when Glenn smiled across at her, Emma said, 'Glenn, why all the questions? Are they why you suggested that we dine out tonight?'

'Not especially. I was just interested, that's all, and felt that you know a lot more about me than I do about you.'

'And does that matter?' Emma asked.

'It might do at some time in the future.'

'Such as…?'

'There are lots of times when the foundations of our lives are of interest to others.'

Emma gave up on that pronouncement and turned her attention to the food, while Glenn reflected that once he had found out the identity of the visitor to her mother's grave and presented them to her, he was going to say something to her that was getting to be long overdue. In the meantime just to have her near was absolutely magical.

When they left the restaurant they walked slowly to the car, holding hands beneath an Easter moon, and Emma's doubts and uncertainties melted away until Glenn pulled up outside her house, kissed her gently on the cheek and said, 'If I'm not around tomorrow, I'll see you at the practice on Tuesday.'

'So you don't want to come in for a coffee?' Emma asked.

Glenn shook his head. 'No, because if I do it will be much more than that I want.' He drove off into the night without further comment, leaving her to wonder what he could possibly mean.

It was busy at the practice on the Tuesday morning after the Easter weekend and Glenn had been hoping that he might have had some good news regarding the long grey raincoat to impart to his father. But ever since Jonas had fallen out of the tree the sun hadn't stopped shining, and there had been no call to ask Emma if she could identify its owner. Besides, Glenn hadn't wanted to mention it to her yet in the vain hope that he might be able to present a complete answer to the question that was eating at him so much.

Quite a few of the regular patients were missing, having been away for the holiday weekend, and as Glenn drove past the mainline railway station on his way back to the practice after a house call in the late morning he saw a few of them homeward bound, unloading themselves and their luggage from a London train. It was then that he spotted the likeable Alex Mowbray amongst them, *and he was wearing a grey belted raincoat.*

As Alex went to join the taxi queue outside the station Glenn pulled up beside him and asked if he wanted a lift, and the offer was gratefully accepted.

'I've been to London a few times over the last couple of months,' Alex explained, as Glenn pulled away from the pavement, 'seeing the shows and generally getting to know the place again after a long absence, but it isn't much fun when one is alone and I'm soon back here in the place I love the most.'

'There is a lot to be said for family life,' Glenn said conversationally. 'I'm fortunate that I still have my parents close by, unlike poor Emma Chalmers—she has no one. Her mother died a few years ago and she has never known who her father is.'

'I hadn't realised that," said Alex. 'Poor Emma, that's very sad.'

'Jeremy Chalmers was Emma's stepfather, he filled the gap left in Emma and Helena's lives when Emma's real father left Helena pregnant, and she never knew the difference. Until in a moment of spite Jeremy enlightened Emma about her true father and she flew the nest to get away from him.'

The colour had drained from the face of the man beside him. 'You are telling me that I have a daughter, is that it?' Alex croaked. 'That I made Helena pregnant on the one and only occasion we made love? It was the night that I was due to leave the UK. I left the next morning to take my sick wife to a gentler climate.

'Helena and I loved each other deeply but my duty was to the woman that I was married to and it was only when she passed away recently that it felt right for me to come back to Glenminster.

'But how did you find out about us? I had prayed that I might find Helena still here and was devastated when it was not to be. I have found solace in putting her favourite flowers on her grave. And then I got to know Emma through your father, with no idea she was my daughter. Glenn, take me to her, please, I beg you!'

Glenn smiled. 'Emma will be busy at the practice at this moment, but if you could wait until tonight I could arrange for the two of you to meet in privacy at my house. It's thanks to my father I've discovered the truth and you have found the daughter you never knew you had.'

'He saw you walking down the road, carrying cream roses, while he was at the top of a tree, trying to get his cat down. He fell off in his excitement and ended up in hospital. But before he fell he noted the raincoat that you're wearing.'

'I can't believe this is happening to me,' Alex said brokenly. 'I have been lonely for so long.'

'Not any more when Emma knows who you are,' Glenn promised. 'Seven o'clock at my place?'

'Yes, absolutely,' Alex agreed, and as his house came into sight he smiled. 'This will be Emma's one day.'

When Glenn arrived back at the practice he told Emma that he would be entertaining a visitor that evening and hoped that she would join them as they would very much like to meet her. Emma's spirits plunged downwards as her first thought was that Glenn had found someone to replace Serena and wanted to break it to her gently.

But she dredged up a smile and asked, 'What time do you want me there?'

'Is seven o'clock all right?'

'Yes, that will be fine,' Emma agreed, and went back to her patients with the thought uppermost in her mind that whatever he had in store for her she would not let him see tears.

When she arrived at the stated time she saw a car on the drive next to his that looked familiar, though she wasn't sure why. Although why it really mattered when she had to get through the evening she didn't know. The sooner this ordeal was over the better.

When Glenn opened the door to her he was smiling, and as she stepped inside he said, 'Someone is waiting to be introduced to you, Emma.' But as she followed him into the sitting room the only person present was Alex Mowbray, who was beaming across at her, and after greeting him she turned to Glenn and said, 'I don't understand. I already know Alex. We are good friends.'

'Er...yes, you do know him,' he agreed. 'You know him as a friend, but Alex is something else as well that you have no idea of. So I'm going to leave him to tell you what that is.' As Emma gazed at him in bewilderment he left them alone with each other and closed the door behind him.

When Glenn had gone, Alex pointed to the sofa and said gently, 'Come and sit by me, Emma, while I tell you something that is wonderful and amazing.' She did as Alex asked, observing him in puzzlement, and he continued, 'I have discovered today from Glenn that we are not just good friends, you and I, but we are also blood relations.'

'How can that be?' Emma asked in amazement. 'I have no family, Alex, none at all.'

'Yes, you have,' Alex said gently. 'Your mother and I loved each other very much, but I had a sick wife I was committed to and Helena and I knew that nothing could come of our love for each other. But on the night before I left this country with my wife, your mother and I slept together.

'I must have made her pregnant, and in keeping with the vows we'd made never to see each other again she didn't get in touch to tell me what had happened. Never betrayed the vow we'd made to keep our love for each other secret for my wife's sake, and it was only today, when Glenn gave me a lift from the station, that my life became worth living again.

'When my wife died only a few months ago I came straight here, but saw the grave and knew I was too late to be with Helena. So I resorted to putting cream roses, her favourite flowers, on it, and would have continued to do so if Glenn's father hadn't seen me on my way there on Good Friday with more flowers. So can you accept me as your father, Emma, someone who will love and cherish you always?'

'Yes, of course,' she said tearfully. 'I have been so lonely, and I liked you from the moment that we met, but never dreamt that we might be related. We have Glenn to thank for this.'

'And my dad, don't forget,' Glenn said, as he came in with flutes of champagne. 'There will be no holding him down after this. So shall we drink to Alex being one of the family and there to give you away, as fathers do, on our wedding day?'

'Yes, please,' she said softly, as all her doubts and fears disappeared, and as they raised their glasses the father that Emma had never known wiped a tear from his eye.

After Alex had gone, quietly radiant, and they were settled in front of the fire, holding hands, Emma said, 'I've thought since we came back from Italy that you were relieved to have an escape route in the form of your father's accident presenting itself to avoid spending time with me, and I am so ashamed.'

'Don't be,' Glenn said gently. 'It was perfectly understandable. The words have been on my lips constantly but I made myself wait until I'd solved the puzzle of the flowers. I can't believe what a wonderful solution it turned out to be.'

'I will never forget that you gave me a family,' Emma said softly, 'and one day hopefully there will be another one, yours and mine, to gladden the hearts of their grandparents. Serena if we have a girl child and Jonas for a boy?'

'Yes, please,' Glenn said, with his arms around her, holding her close in what felt like the safest place on earth. 'And I have some more news concerning Dad. Mum rang earlier to say that he has been discharged from the hospital. They let her take him home with her after this evening's visiting.

'Shall we go round there and tell them the good news that Alex is going to be part of the family for evermore, and that one day they may be granted their greatest wish of the patter of tiny feet all around them?'

'Yes,' Emma said joyfully. 'Your father deserves to hear something good after what happened to him, and your mother will be delighted to know that you and I love each other, and that we are going to spend the rest of our lives together.'

'You came out of nowhere and captured my heart, brought me joy out of sadness at Christmastime,' Glenn told her. 'Would you be prepared to wait until it comes round again for a Christmas wedding?'

'Yes, that would be lovely,' Emma said without hesitation, smiling up at him with the promise of all the happiness to come in her bright hazel gaze, 'just as long as I can live here with you from this day on, which is something I've always wanted.'

'That goes without saying,' he said tenderly. 'Where else would I want you to be but in my home, in my heart?'

When his parents had heard all their news, they rejoiced to hear that not only was Alex Emma's father but he would be at the engagement party that the two doctors were planning on having with family, friends and the practice staff in the near future. It seemed that Jonas's glimpse of him before the branch had given way had provided the answer to the mystery of the cream roses, and in spite of his injuries he was a very happy man.

Emma and Glenn had decided to hold their engagement party at Glenn's house with outside caterers in charge of refreshments. When they went into work the next day they amazed everyone except Lydia by announcing their engagement and inviting them to celebrate it with them some time in the near future. For the rest of the day it was the main topic of conversation.

That evening, wanting to have all ends tied up of what was going to be one of the happiest times of his life, Glenn said, 'What kind of a ring would you like, Emma? Something other than that ill-fated solitaire diamond that I made such a hash of when I produced it?'

Emma smiled across at him. 'I would like the diamond if you still have it,' she said softly. When Glenn looked at her in surprise she added, 'I have realised since that the way you explained it when you offered it to me was because you cared about me, and needed to make me see how much you would never want to let your painful past hurt me as it hurts you. I misjudged you, Glenn. So if you still have it, that is the ring I would like to wear.'

'You are incredible,' he said gently, 'and, yes, I have still got it in a drawer in my bedroom, so shall I go and get it?'

'Yes, please,' Emma told him, happy that the dark moment from the past was turning into a joyful one, and when Glenn took her hand and placed the sparkling ring on her finger, there was brightness all around them.

The engagement party was like a dream coming true for them as they greeted their guests on an evening in early June, and when Alex arrived and held her close for a fatherly moment, Emma's contentment was complete.

She had been round to his place on a few occasions to get to know him and it was always a time of fulfilment and thankfulness when she thought of how Glenn had brought him to her out of nowhere and into her life.

It seemed that Alex had been the bank manager of one of the biggest banks in Glenminster and Helena had been his secretary. They had fallen deeply in love with the knowledge that there had been no future for them to be together because Alex had been unable to leave his sick wife, and she, Emma, had been the result of wishing each other a passionate goodbye.

But a warm June night with love in the air and lots of nice food and wine to partake of in the company of friends was not the occasion for sad memories, and when Glenn asked Emma if she was happy, the answer was there in her eyes and the tender curve of her mouth, and as Lydia watched them she felt a rush of thankfulness in knowing that there was a happy ending for Emma's hurts of long ago.

EPILOGUE

CHRISTMAS HAD COME again and in the ancient church next to the practice the wedding march was being played as Emma walked slowly along the aisle in a dress of heavy cream brocade designed to keep out the cold, carrying a bouquet of roses of the same colour. She was holding onto the arm of her father, who was observing her with loving pride and joy as the solitaire diamond on her finger sparkled in the light of many candles.

All around them was the Yuletide smell of fresh green spruces and as Glenn stood waiting for her at the altar he sent up a silent prayer of thankfulness for the joy she had brought into his life and the lives of others, including that of his elderly best man, who had risked life and limb on their account.

Tonight he would keep the promise he had made to Emma at the side of the empty hayloft that day. There had been times over recent months when it had been a hard promise to keep, but tonight when they were alone Glenn would show her how much he loved her and always would.

And as Emma came to stand beside him, looking beautiful beyond telling, he felt Serena's presence, as he sometimes did, close by and peaceful in the ether, and contentment filled his heart as he and Emma made the vows that would last a lifetime.

They were going to honeymoon in Italy in the beautiful house where they had stayed so briefly before the phone call from Glenn's mother had brought them swiftly back home. But on this occasion they fully intended to enjoy the beauties of the coastline, now that they had all the time in the world to adore each other. And on their return to Glenminster there would be all the things that were precious in their lives waiting for them.

Such as their parents, Glenn's house, which Emma had adored ever since she'd first seen it, and their all-consuming work at the practice amongst the sick and suffering, with their love for each other their strength in all things.

* * * * *

MILLS & BOON®
Hardback – December 2015

ROMANCE

The Price of His Redemption	Carol Marinelli
Back in the Brazilian's Bed	Susan Stephens
The Innocent's Sinful Craving	Sara Craven
Brunetti's Secret Son	Maya Blake
Talos Claims His Virgin	Michelle Smart
Destined for the Desert King	Kate Walker
Ravensdale's Defiant Captive	Melanie Milburne
Caught in His Gilded World	Lucy Ellis
The Best Man & The Wedding Planner	Teresa Carpenter
Proposal at the Winter Ball	Jessica Gilmore
Bodyguard...to Bridegroom?	Nikki Logan
Christmas Kisses with Her Boss	Nina Milne
Playboy Doc's Mistletoe Kiss	Tina Beckett
Her Doctor's Christmas Proposal	Louisa George
From Christmas to Forever?	Marion Lennox
A Mummy to Make Christmas	Susanne Hampton
Miracle Under the Mistletoe	Jennifer Taylor
His Christmas Bride-to-Be	Abigail Gordon
Lone Star Holiday Proposal	Yvonne Lindsay
A Baby for the Boss	Maureen Child

MILLS & BOON®
Large Print – December 2015

ROMANCE

The Greek Demands His Heir	Lynne Graham
The Sinner's Marriage Redemption	Annie West
His Sicilian Cinderella	Carol Marinelli
Captivated by the Greek	Julia James
The Perfect Cazorla Wife	Michelle Smart
Claimed for His Duty	Tara Pammi
The Marakaios Baby	Kate Hewitt
Return of the Italian Tycoon	Jennifer Faye
His Unforgettable Fiancée	Teresa Carpenter
Hired by the Brooding Billionaire	Kandy Shepherd
A Will, a Wish...a Proposal	Jessica Gilmore

HISTORICAL

Griffin Stone: Duke of Decadence	Carole Mortimer
Rake Most Likely to Thrill	Bronwyn Scott
Under a Desert Moon	Laura Martin
The Bootlegger's Daughter	Lauri Robinson
The Captain's Frozen Dream	Georgie Lee

MEDICAL

Midwife...to Mum!	Sue MacKay
His Best Friend's Baby	Susan Carlisle
Italian Surgeon to the Stars	Melanie Milburne
Her Greek Doctor's Proposal	Robin Gianna
New York Doc to Blushing Bride	Janice Lynn
Still Married to Her Ex!	Lucy Clark

MILLS & BOON®
Hardback – January 2016

ROMANCE

The Queen's New Year Secret	Maisey Yates
Wearing the De Angelis Ring	Cathy Williams
The Cost of the Forbidden	Carol Marinelli
Mistress of His Revenge	Chantelle Shaw
Theseus Discovers His Heir	Michelle Smart
The Marriage He Must Keep	Dani Collins
Awakening the Ravensdale Heiress	Melanie Milburne
New Year at the Boss's Bidding	Rachael Thomas
His Princess of Convenience	Rebecca Winters
Holiday with the Millionaire	Scarlet Wilson
The Husband She'd Never Met	Barbara Hannay
Unlocking Her Boss's Heart	Christy McKellen
A Daddy for Baby Zoe?	Fiona Lowe
A Love Against All Odds	Emily Forbes
Her Playboy's Proposal	Kate Hardy
One Night...with Her Boss	Annie O'Neil
A Mother for His Adopted Son	Lynne Marshall
A Kiss to Change Her Life	Karin Baine
Twin Heirs to His Throne	Olivia Gates
A Baby for the Boss	Maureen Child

MILLS & BOON®
Large Print – January 2016

ROMANCE

The Greek Commands His Mistress	Lynne Graham
A Pawn in the Playboy's Game	Cathy Williams
Bound to the Warrior King	Maisey Yates
Her Nine Month Confession	Kim Lawrence
Traded to the Desert Sheikh	Caitlin Crews
A Bride Worth Millions	Chantelle Shaw
Vows of Revenge	Dani Collins
Reunited by a Baby Secret	Michelle Douglas
A Wedding for the Greek Tycoon	Rebecca Winters
Beauty & Her Billionaire Boss	Barbara Wallace
Newborn on Her Doorstep	Ellie Darkins

HISTORICAL

Marriage Made in Shame	Sophia James
Tarnished, Tempted and Tamed	Mary Brendan
Forbidden to the Duke	Liz Tyner
The Rebel Daughter	Lauri Robinson
Her Enemy Highlander	Nicole Locke

MEDICAL

Unlocking Her Surgeon's Heart	Fiona Lowe
Her Playboy's Secret	Tina Beckett
The Doctor She Left Behind	Scarlet Wilson
Taming Her Navy Doc	Amy Ruttan
A Promise...to a Proposal?	Kate Hardy
Her Family for Keeps	Molly Evans

MILLS & BOON®

Why shop at millsandboon.co.uk?

Each year, thousands of romance readers find their perfect read at millsandboon.co.uk. That's because we're passionate about bringing you the very best romantic fiction. Here are some of the advantages of shopping at www.millsandboon.co.uk:

* **Get new books first**—you'll be able to buy your favourite books one month before they hit the shops

* **Get exclusive discounts**—you'll also be able to buy our specially created monthly collections, with up to 50% off the RRP

* **Find your favourite authors**—latest news, interviews and new releases for all your favourite authors and series on our website, plus ideas for what to try next

* **Join in**—once you've bought your favourite books, don't forget to register with us to rate, review and join in the discussions

Visit **www.millsandboon.co.uk**
for all this and more today!